"Somebody's be_____
hut. See how the ta_____

Scott Jenkins loo_____
for arrowheads. "Who would that be, Johnny?"

"Might be easier to tell you who it ought not be, which is NOBODY." I thought of what Pa told me the night before, turning my jubilant homecoming to gloom. From then on, my mind had been trapped in a dark hole of misery.

My sigh came out deep enough to blow gnats from my face. "Pa says that with more and more strangers coming up on this here mountain, you can't tell what any one of 'em might do, or where he's likely to go. There's been stealing going on."

Willis Thompson pushed up his glasses, which are so thick they make his eyes look like two big bomber marbles. "It's happening all over, guys. My dad told me there's been a string of robberies in town, too."

I moved to lead the way down the path. "Something rotten's operating on Mirror Mountain, for certain."

In memory of my mother and father
and all the other good people of my growing-up
days
who shared with me their richest blessings:
Faith, Hope, Love, and Joy.

Not what we give, but what we share,
For the gift without the giver is bare
Who gives himself with his alms feeds three—
Himself, his hungering neighbor, and me.

James Russell Lowell
(1819-1891)

A MIRROR MOUNTAIN ADVENTURE

INVASION
ON MIRROR MOUNTAIN

WYNNETTE FRASER

Chariot Books™
David C. Cook Publishing Co.

Chariot Books™ is an imprint of
David C. Cook Publishing Co.
David C. Cook Publishing Co., Elgin, Illinois 60120
David C. Cook Publishing Co., Weston, Ontario
Nova Distribution Ltd., Newton Abbot, England

INVASION ON MIRROR MOUNTAIN
© 1994 by Wynnette Fraser

Scripture quotations are from The Living Bible, © 1971,
Tyndale House Publishers, Wheaton, IL 60187. Used by
permission.

Cover illustration by Wendy Wassink Ackison
First Printing, 1994
Printed in the United States of America
98 97 96 95 94 5 4 3 2 1

Library of Congress Cataloging-in-Publication Data
Fraser, Wynnette, 1925-
Invasion on Mirror Mountain / by Wynnette Fraser.
           pm.   cm.
Summary: When a construction project brings an army of strangers onto his
mountain, twelve-year-old Johnny wonders if one of them may be
responsible for the flurry of thefts in the area.
ISBN 0-7814-0104-6
[1. Mountain life—Fiction. 2. Christian life—Fiction. 3. Mystery and
detective stories.] I. Title.
PZ7.F8647In 1994
[Fic]—dc20   93-32678
                                                        CIP
                                                        AC

Contents

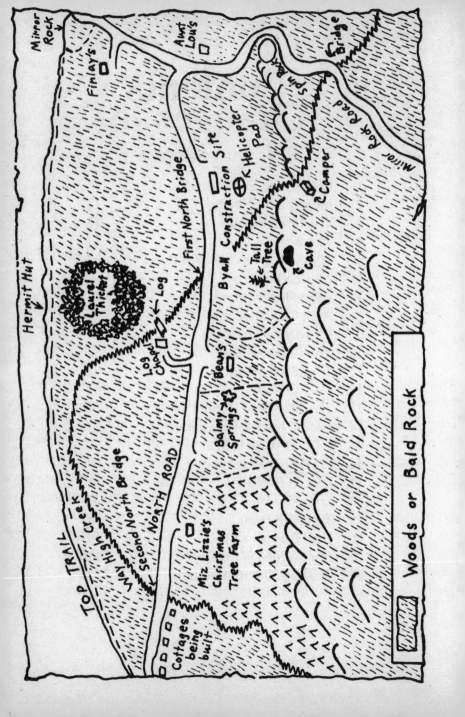

Mirror Rock

Finlay's

Aunt Lou's

Bridge

Hermit Hut

Helicopter Pad

First North Bridge

Byall Construction Site

Spring Bank

Mirror Rock Road

Camper

Tall Tree

Cave

Log Chapel

Log

Laurel Thicket

Bean's

Balmy Springs

TOP TRAIL

High Creek

Way

Second North Bridge

NORTH ROAD

Miz Lizzie's

Christmas Tree Farm

Cottages being built

Woods or Bald Rock

1
Changes to Explore

"Somebody's been using our path to the hermit hut. See how the tall weeds are all squashed down?"

Scott Jenkins looked up from scanning the ground for arrowheads. "Who would that be, Johnny?"

My full name is Johnny Elbert Finlay, but most folks call me Johnny. "Might be easier to tell you who it ought not be, which is NOBODY." I thought of what Pa told me the night before, turning my jubilant homecoming to gloom. From then on, my mind had been trapped in a dark hole of misery.

My sigh came out deep enough to blow gnats from my face. "Pa says that with more and more strangers coming up on this here mountain, you can't tell what any one of 'em might do, or where he's likely to go. There's been stealing going on."

Willis Thompson pushed up his glasses, which are so thick they make his eyes look like two big bomber marbles. "It's happening all over, guys. My dad told me there's been a string of robberies in town, too."

I moved to lead the way down the path. "Something rotten's operating on Mirror Mountain, for certain." I pushed a strip of hay-brown hair from my forehead. "Last night, when Louise and I got home from Deepwood Bay, Pa told us the church's new sound system got stolen."

Scott frowned. "Who'd rob a church!"

Willis said, "My dad thinks someone smart is behind the town robberies. The police can't seem to catch them."

Scott slapped his cheek. "What if we Hermiteers get to our clubhouse and find a robber or two hiding out there?"

It had been with me since we stepped off Top Trail—a creepy feeling that unseen eyes were watching us. But I wouldn't mention it till I was sure it wasn't just my mind doing a number on me.

"Maybe it was just a harmless animal using our path," Willis said with a shrug.

"Probably so," I agreed. "I reckon even the critters done got all shook up over all the changes taking place up here."

"Changes?" Scott questioned.

"Yep. Some are good. You saw how Mirror Rock Road's smoothed out to be paved. And with our new phone, I got you guys up here the first day after I came home from Wistero Island."

"Sure did," Scott said. "Did you have fun on the island?"

The backpack was getting heavy, and we were breathing faster. "Sure did. Later, I'll tell you all that happened, like I want you to tell me about Camp Walking Tall. Right now, soon's we check on the hut, we need to start on our way to Balmy Springs."

"Balmy Springs?" the two boys said together.

Midnight, Aunt Lou's big black dog, bumped me and ran ahead down the path. I turned and signed the boys to stop for a couple minutes' rest.

"It's down North Road," I explained, "and I definitely want to go there."

"What's happening down North Road?"

"According to my pa, development. Some rich man's got ahold of Corn Kelly's old place. Pa says the same man also went and bought some government land. That's further down, past Miz Lizzie West's Christmas tree farm."

"The same Miz Lizzie you told me about, the one with the Civil War gun?" Willis patted a camera that hung on a strap from his shoulder. "I took photography at camp. Do you think she'd let me take a picture of that gun?"

"Maybe. Miz Lizzie's mighty proud of all them old family treasures that came down to her."

It was plain that Scott had something else he wanted to talk about. "Johnny, let's get back to Corn Kelly. How did he sell his property? I thought he was in prison for growing marijuana."

"You got it. But according to Pa, he went without

9

paying his overdue taxes." I kicked at some weeds in the path. "Corn's property went up for auction."

"Didn't he have any family to stop that from happening?" Willis asked.

"Just a puny little wife. Corn didn't even list her on the deed, Pa says. When he went to the pen, Maybelle went back to her folks and didn't leave any address."

We started back to walking. I could see Midnight at the big boulders ahead. He seemed to be waiting for us.

"Well, who bought it?" Scott asked.

"Pa said the highest bidder was the owner of Sweet South Beverages in Greenville."

"Oh, I know who that is," Willis said. "His name's Will Byall. He came to our house once, to see Dad about some legal matter. What's he going to do with all that property?"

"Pa says they're building houses on what's down past Miz Lizzie's. As for Corn's place, Pa heard tell it's gonna be a plant to bottle up mountain water for to sell."

"My mom might like that idea," said Scott. "She says water's better for me than Sweet Zingy Punch."

I shook my head. "It ain—isn't good news to us mountaineers. If they tap the water sources in them rocks, Balmy Springs could dry up."

"The same Balmy Springs we're going to?"

"I reckon I never told you about all the springs 'round about Corn's place. Balmy Springs, the main one, is between his place and Miz Lizzie's. But Byall didn't get his hands on that one. No siree. Awhile back, our church folks went together and bought the hollow it's in. They say it's God's water because sick people get healed when they drink it."

We reached the tall boulders, which we had to go around to get to the east ledge where the hermit hut was.

I halted. "Where's Midnight?" It was like the big black dog had disappeared right in front of my eyes.

"Bet he went ahead of us to chase the thieves away from our hut," Willis suggested.

His light remark pointed me to a fact I should not have forgotten. If strangers were spying on us, any dog would sniff them out and bark, wouldn't he? It eased my mind a bit.

"With Midnight's help, we three Hermiteers might catch a ring of thieves all by ourselves!" bragged Scott.

If I'd been ten years old like Scott and Willis, I might have said "yeah" to that. But I was almost thirteen, and had to act more grown-up.

"That ain—isn't likely to happen," I told them. "Our clubhouse is barely big enough for a hermit to hide."

When we made it around the rocks, we found the east ledge was deserted. Hermit Dan's old hut still stood against the shoulder of rock which was also its rear wall.

After we set down our backpacks, Scott got out his binoculars and looked off the cliff.

Willis went straight to shooting pictures. He stood, squatted and kneeled, nodding or shaking his round head. K-REEH K-REEH went the camera.

The meadow that sloped away from the ledge looked almost the same in late August as it had last spring. Curly green vines looked downright thankful for last night's rain. I was just glad that Will Byall didn't own this part of the mountain—yet.

I whistled for Midnight, but he didn't come. Why couldn't that dog stay put till I checked inside the hut? I tried to shove aside the creepy feeling that was coming back to me, and went over to the hut.

I yanked at the rusty screen door, expecting to find it stuck tight from the rain. It wasn't, and that speeded up my heart rate. Go easy, now.

Scott was right behind me, and I waved him back.

"You w-wait out there with Willis. Don't come in till I holler 'okay.' But if I yell 'RUN,' both of you guys beat it for Top Trail and don't stop till you get help."

With shoulders stiff as two fence posts, I bit my lip and gave the wooden door a quick jerk.

WHAM-A-LAM. A clanging noise hit my ears, and something swung out and whacked me on the forehead. "OUCH!" I bellowed, batting my eyes like a toad in a hailstorm.

I felt hands pushing at my shoulders.

2
Men and Machines

Scott and Willis were trying to stumble over me to see what had happened.

"I told you guys to wait!" I barked, rubbing my head and blinking my eyes.

"But you didn't say 'run' or 'okay,' " Scott reminded. "How were we to know what to do with 'OUCH'?"

Then those two goons started laughing to beat forty.

"Look what you ran into, Johnny!"

Willis pointed to a string of tin cans swinging over the inside door. Somebody had it fixed to come down on whoever pushed the door open. The edge of one had caught me just above the eye, but the pain was already gone. I took a quick look around the room and was glad to feel foolish. Whoever had fixed that little welcome trap was not in the clubhouse now.

Sunlight streaked through the door like a yellow butterfly. It lit on the wooden box lying sidelong in the center of the room. When Hermit Dan was alive, that box had been his table. Now we called it ours. On it was a zinc bucket, gourd dipper, and speckled basin.

Scott crinkled up his nose, sniffing equal to Midnight. "This place smells fresh," he said. "I thought we'd have to air it out again."

I sniffed and frowned. "Too fresh."

"Hey, guys, take a look at this," piped Willis, peering through his thick glasses at a rusty can on the box. Bright yellow daisies spilled over its sides.

Willis stuck a finger in the can. "Fresh wildflowers in a full can of fresh water!" He held up his wet finger for us to see.

Fresh water? That didn't make sense, and I said as much. "Remember how we had to tote jugs of water up here last May? Almost every day it was, till Charley Hawk's sprained wing healed."

"Sure do," said Scott. "We wondered then why Hermit Dan didn't build his hut closer to the creek."

Willis scratched his head. "But Hermit Dan's been dead for years, and Charley Hawk's flying free. So who'd be stupid enough to haul creek water just to keep wildflowers fresh?"

Scott batted his eyes like a flirty girl. Slowly, he shook a finger at Willis, who is not sloppy like Scott and me.

This time he balled his fists against his hips and glared at us. "Definitely, positively, absolutely, and totally—NOT!"

14

Scott raised his eyebrows and rolled his eyes my way. "Johnny, you could have . . ."

"Aw, knock it off," I said with a snort. "None of us would do such a dumb thing. Besides, the last time any of us were here was the week after school let out."

"That's right," Willis remembered. "The answer is obvious enough. A girl has invaded our clubhouse."

"A—a girl?" I stammered. "Nary a girl knows about this place. Well, not unless you count my sister. But Louise was gone all summer, same as the rest of us."

Willis aimed his camera at the flowers. The bright flash almost blinded us. He eyed our dogwood broom that stood in the corner. "Evidence of invasion," he muttered. "I'm positive I left that broom over the rafters last spring. . . ." K-RRR-EEH K-RRR-EEH went the camera as the flash lit up the hut again.

Scott reared back and shoved his hands into his pockets. "Look at it this way," he said. "At least the prowler aired out our clubhouse."

"Seems so," I muttered, "but according to mountain law, this hut belongs to us Hermiteers. Some stranger has come up here and trespassed."

Since Willis's dad is a lawyer, he felt obliged to put in his two cents. "According to federal law," he put forth, "we may be trespassers ourselves, on government property."

"I don't see any 'no trespassing' signs," said Scott. "That means the public's free to come here.

Besides, the hut's not damaged, just invaded."

I shrugged. "I reckon not. I just wonder who found the way here. The path is hid real good from Top Trail hikers."

"The thieves, maybe?" Willis frowned. "Nothing here is worth stealing."

"I still say only a girl would bother to put flowers here," Scott declared.

I took a deep breath. "Maybe, but let it go for now. How 'bout us starting our hike down North Road?"

I made sure both doors to the hermit hut were closed tight. With our backpacks strapped on, we backtracked down the same path to Top Trail.

We crossed the trail and went down into a ravine, then up and out of it. From there to Way High Creek, the mountain slope was spread with a green blanket of laurel bushes.

Willis had never squirreled through a laurel thicket before, so Scott and I showed him how. He couldn't get over how soon we made it to Way High Creek, going from one limb to the next.

We came out across the creek from the log chapel, and I led the boys along the side we were on, toward First North Bridge.

Soon Midnight was back, splashing and slushing his long black nose through the creek shallows. It eased my mind to watch him cavort like a frisky pup.

What didn't ease my mind a skinny bit was the unseemly racket our ears were now picking up. We could no longer hear the birds singing. Even the bushes seemed to shiver. Loud, grinding sounds drowned out the whisper of the creek.

We scrambled up the bank beside the bridge. Ahead of us, across the road and up a little hill, the noisemakers came into view.

I could hardly believe what was happening on my mountain. Men, trucks, bulldozers, and draglines were everywhere. Gone were most of the trees from both sides of the creek that ran through what was Corn Kelly's woods. It sure looked like men were building Byall's water-bottling plant.

A neat-looking stranger stood in front of a trailer marked OFFICE, watching the workmen. He was older than Pa, and had gray sideburns that matched his trim little moustache. His face was a bit wrinkled, but his work clothes were clean and smooth.

Pa says even if we don't take kindly to strangers, that's no call to be unfriendly. Friendly or not, I kept Midnight close to my side as we moseyed over to say howdy. "Are you Mr. Byall?" I asked him right off.

He tweaked his moustache and gave us a slit-eyed look. "If I were Will Byall, would I stand here sweating? No, I'd be in my air-conditioned office in Greenville, which is probably where he sits right now." He mopped his forehead with a handkerchief. "I'm Sam Grove, the foreman.

We told him our names. "We're a mite curious about this place, Mr. Grove," I said.

"Are, huh? Well, as you can see, the big building going up will be stone-covered. And over yonder where they've cleared away the trees, that's a landing pad for helicopters. Getting here in a hurry will be a cinch for the big boys."

So what Pa had heard must be true. Those "big boys" were bound to be money hogs who wouldn't give a rip about ruining my mountain.

"Don't see why you had to knock down all them trees," I told him point-blank.

"I see why," Scott butted in to say. "Helicopters need plenty of open space around the landing pad."

"Your buddy's right," Mr. Grove told me. "And you also got to clear wooded land to put up buildings, kid."

"My name's Johnny. Buildings go up fast, Mr. Grove, but you see that great big chestnut oak they're cutting up over there? It's been a'growing nigh on to a hundred years or so."

Sam Grove's glance followed mine toward the tree. The tree's big stump was fast turning to sawdust, thanks to a noisy stump-grinding machine. "Your tree won't grow no more," said Grove. "That's progress, kid."

"Johnny," I reminded him, a bit curtly.

"Er—uhh, Johnny, then." He shrugged his big shoulders. Then he turned from us to scowl at a workman who stood in dry pine straw, smoking a cigarette.

"Boozer," he yelled, "be careful with that cigarette."

When the man acted like he didn't hear, Grove walked over to him. "You've run out of break time, Booze. I told you not to push me too far on this job. Go help Potter with the stones he's laying."

Boozer was naked from the waist up. He should have covered up those bony ribs and shoulders. A mud-brown bushy beard jutted out from his chin. His long hair, also mud-brown, was bunched into a ponytail. If a strong wind had come along and flipped it up, we'd have been hard put to tell if he was coming or going.

Boozer shrugged, dropped the cigarette butt and wiggled his shoe over it, not hurrying to get around the corner of the building.

In the next minute or two, a lean, dark-haired man in muddy coveralls came around the same corner. The trowel he toted tipped me off that he was the man called Potter. "I SENT BOOZER TO LOAD TREES," he yelled. "I DON'T NEED HIS HELP."

Sam Grove signed agreement and heaved a wearisome sigh as Potter went back around the corner.

"We'll be going now. Sorry I couldn't talk to Mr. Byall."

He nodded absent-like, and we headed north towards Balmy Springs.

"I don't think Mr. Grove likes his job," Willis said.

Scott shrugged. "No wonder, with someone like Boozer to oversee. My dad wouldn't keep a worker like that."

"Don't sound to me like Byall cares what's going on up here," I said, frowning. "Just sends a bunch of strangers to hack it all up. I aim to be a conservationist, but I got to grow up and get my schooling first. That'll be too late for me to save the trees or the wildlife."

"Sure looks that way," agreed Willis. "It's terrible for them to cut all those trees. I know how bad it must make you feel, Johnny."

I looked away from the boys. "No, you d-don't know," I said, blinking hard to keep from crying. "Nobody can know, less'n they been part of a mountain all their lives."

"I don't guess they can," Willis said, "I suppose it gets to fit a guy like his clothes."

"Better'n that," I came back, "it hangs on me lots better'n this shirt I got on."

Scott chuckled. "Johnny, anything would hang better than that big T-shirt," he said. "Where can I get one like it?"

My mood lightened a bit. "Don't even think about it," I quipped. "This here's a Super-Sam original," I caught up my shirttail and did a show-off strut, which was good for a laugh.

We kept to the road and came to Corn's old dirt driveway. It winds up and over a wooded hill, then down into a hollow you can't see from the road. Scott started to turn onto it.

"Hold up," I told him. "Balmy Springs turnoff is the next one."

Scott sighed. "Super. I'm getting so hungry, I could eat a humongous alien from outer space. I sure hope you brought some homemade brownies, Johnny."

"Yeah. But Ma made me promise we'd finish our sandwiches first." Scott loves Ma's brownies. In fact, he loves almost anything that's okay to eat, plus some foods I wouldn't touch with a ten-foot pole.

When we reached Balmy Springs, Midnight had run off somewhere again. We walked down the cedar-lined driveway that hides Balmy Springs Hollow from the road, and reached the parking lot near the spring.

The spring itself flows from a cluster of rocks that are ten feet high. It flows out through a pipe someone set near the bottom of the rocks.

Folks also built a low rock wall around the spring pool. They left an opening near the top of it for the clear water to spill over into a gully that trickles into the woods.

A black locust post was sunk beside the pool, with hooks that held three gourd dippers. We used them to catch and drink the cool water.

On one of the tables was a tin can with flowers like those in the hermit hut.

"Well, how 'bout that," Scott said. "It looks like the flower girl decorated our banquet table."

"Well, she might've at least cleaned the mud off it," said Willis.

"Aw, I'm ready to eat now," Scott said. "Let's just spread our lunch on another table."

I bit into my sandwich, but those flowers puzzled me. Plainly they were put here by whoever invaded our hut and set up the trap to spook us. Would a tough thief bother with such silly, frilly doings? Not if he was all there, I decided.

3
The Little People

I opened my peanut butter and jelly sandwich, and got a whiff of roasted peanuts that made me forget all my complaints.

Midnight showed up long enough to get what handouts we could spare, then left again.

As we swapped stories about the fun we had each had during the summer, I saw something move at the top of the high rock behind the spring.

Quick as a flash, a teeny head ducked behind a bush. From another bush, a second head popped up and out of sight.

I lowered my voice. "Don't look now," I said, "but some short people's up there spying on us."

Of course they looked, but saw nothing.

"Maybe there are little people in your woods," said Willis. "You know, fairies, gnomes, leprechauns." His voice was low and eerie sounding.

Scott's eyes glowed. "Or naughty little banshees! Let's go up and flush 'em out."

"Okay," I said, "but we'll have to circle back by Corn Kelly's place to get up there."

"Let's do it," Scott urged.

Willis agreed. I went along with the idea because I was more than a little curious myself.

We finished our lunch, except for the dozen brownies in a zip bag inside my backpack.

"Let's hide our packs under them shrubs over yonder till we come back," I said.

"What about the brownies?" Scott wanted to know.

"They'll keep. Right now, I'm full as a June goat, and you oughta be, too."

"I guess." Scott reached over and patted the little bump our dessert made through the canvas of my pack. "You sweet little morsels," he cooed. "You stay right here till we get back."

If that didn't beat all, him talking to food! I screwed up my face at him and quickly shoved the backpack out of sight.

Back at Corn's driveway, we noticed tire tracks in the dirt.

Willis bent his head for a better look. "These were made by a truck." He straightened up. "Yes, I would say these are definitely truck tire tracks."

Corn Kelly's homeplace was one part of the mountain I didn't know very well. Except when Pa took me there, I had always gone out of my way to stay clear of it. I never could figure how Pa put up with a moonshinin' partner so mean and low-down as Corn. Of course, that was before Pa found the Lord and totally quit making bootleg whiskey.

24

Thank goodness the old bully was now in prison for fifteen years. Whatever we found over that little hill, it couldn't be as bad as running into Corn Kelly.

In short order, we halted at the crest of the hill. The driveway sloped down away from us, ending at Corn's old shack at the far end of the hollow. But something strange was sitting between us and the shack.

It was a great big old school bus with curtained windows. Beside the bus, a canvas canopy shaded a table with straight folding chairs around it.

Water bubbled from two hillside springs into one shallow pool. Judging from where they were, I figured they were fed by the same underground stream that kept Balmy Springs going. I reckon I never noticed that when I went there with Pa.

There was a clothesline with a pair of man-sized coveralls hanging on it. Alongside that were underclothes that went from big to little. Of course, strangers come in all sizes.

No stranger was showing just then, but as we walked along, I felt we were being watched.

All three of us had our eyes on the bus. All of us saw the curtain move. And the split second that it slid from behind the curtain, every one of us saw the gleaming barrel of a gun. It was pointed straight at us.

"DON'T COME ANY CLOSER OR I MIGHT SHOOT!" yelled a half-grown voice.

Midnight picked that minute to show up and bumped against me. I grabbed his collar and tried to sign warnings to the others. But I lost my grip on his collar, and the dog bounded for the nearby woods.

4
The Beans

It was like my feet were glued to the ground, and my mouth was sewed up tight. "Please, Lord, I'm too young to die," I prayed.

The next second or two seemed to poke along like dust on a turtle's back. I cut an eye at Willis. His mouth was stuck on OPEN, and his eyes looked like two big marbles that were mostly white.

As I cranked up for a fast turn-and-run, it dawned on me that Scott was still walking forward. Raising both hands high in the air, he yelled, "WE COME IN PEACE. LET'S TALK THIS OVER."

My friend was either real brave or real stupid. Whichever it was, I felt obliged to act fast. Somehow, I switched my feet to fast forward and got between Scott and the pointed weapon.

"YOU IN THERE, WE AIN'T L-LOOKING FOR TROUBLE." I tried to work a growl into my shaky voice. "M-MY FAMILY'S BEEN A'LIVING ON THIS MOUNTAIN NIGH ONTO 200 YEARS." I said all that so fast, my words ran together.

The gun barrel slid back out of sight. I inhaled a

thankful gulp of air, and let it shiver its way out of my mouth.

A gangly boy about fifteen or so came out, unarmed. He looked familiar, but I didn't know why. He was long and lean, with straight, dark hair and a face that didn't try to smile.

I walked over to shake hands, but his hands stayed on his hips, so I just told him our names, and asked him to tell us his.

He fastened me with a grim look. "Wylie Bean, and I'll thank you to state your business here."

Huffy orders tend to bring out the Finlay stubbornness in me. Without his gun, I banked on the guy being mostly mouth. "How long you been here?" I asked him.

"You're nosy as that fat woman down the road," he snapped.

"If you mean Miz Lizzie West, I doubt it." Soon as I said it, I knew I'd gone and shot off my mouth without thinking. Ma would be hurt over my speaking unkindly of a neighbor, but everybody knows Miz Lizzie's parakeet nose twists up, down, and sideways, sniffing out rumors to spread around. "But Miz Lizzie's not a bad person," I finished.

"Maybe not," his voice was calmer, "but she ought to mind her own business like we do."

"You shouldn't be pointing guns at people," Scott ventured to say. "You could kill someone like that."

The boy shrugged. "Got a right to protect my

28

property, don't I? You ought not sneak up like that."

"I thought all this land belonged to Mr. Will Byall now," said Willis.

"Not these four acres. Dad bought them from Mr. Byall. I'm in charge here while Dad's laying stone at the construction site."

"Is he the one called Potter?" asked Scott.

Wylie nodded. "Real name's Pothorf, but he hates it. He likes to be called Potter because that's what he really is—a country potter." He pointed to Corn's old shack that pretty much sits on the ground. "I turn pots and jugs too. See those over there on the porch?"

We could see them all right, red clay jugs and pots. "Looks like you put some new boards around them doors and windows," I said. "You live in it too?"

"Nah. For now we live in the bus. We hope to build a house later, but the shack's gonna be our pottery. When Dad's construction job runs out, we aim to get it going full-time."

"My cousin Teal Finlay's got a pottery," I said. "It's set up in a big old barn off the Blue Ridge Parkway."

Wylie shrugged. "Well, ours is all set up, and we got the stones to finish our curing kiln, piled up out back. Dad just has weekends to work on it."

"Won't it be hard to find customers way up here?" Scott asked.

"Dad says when all the building's over with, this mountain'll be jumping with vacation people. He says they'll be coming right to our door."

"I just hope you don't go pointing that gun at your customers," Scott said.

A devilish grin crawled over Wylie's face. "Oh, that's not a real gun," he said. "It's just a half-inch pipe I keep inside. If I'd thought you guys were real trouble, I'd have loaded Dad's shotgun before coming out."

I traded sheepish looks with Scott and Willis. Wylie Bean had fooled us good. Maybe he had it in him to fix that trap at the hut, only I couldn't see him fixing flowers.

"Callie! Coyt!" Wylie suddenly yelled toward a clump of myrtles up the hill by the driveway. "I know you're there, so come on out!"

We turned to see the bushes part. I thought I was seeing double. Two children with dirty faces and clothes came lickety-split down the hill. Alongside them ran Midnight, doing a dance of circles.

About ten feet away from us, the younguns stopped and stared. Both looked to be about six years old, and had short, dark hair.

Midnight began to lick what looked like mud from their cheeks, but Wylie got onto the younguns about running off, and sent them to wash up. "Coyt and Callie are twins," he told us. "I think that black dog shows 'em places to run off to."

"He's my Aunt Lou's dog," I said. "Name's Midnight."

"Come on, Midnight," Coyt called. The dog splashed into the spring pool alongside the twins. They giggled and squealed as Midnight yipped like he was half his age.

Wylie shook his head. "Two tornadoes," he said. "They need to be spanked, but I'm not allowed to, and Dad won't."

"What about your mom?" Willis asked.

Wylie's face clouded up. "Sh-she's away. Hey, what is this? Am I in court?" It was plain we had asked one too many questions.

"We better go now," I said. "If you get a mind to come visit, I live with my folks up Mirror Rock Road."

"Thanks, but I stay pretty busy. Later, maybe."

As we walked over the hill again, Scott said, "Gee, that Wylie turned out to be sort of nice, after all."

"Nice, but sad," said Willis.

I kicked a big pinecone out of my way. "With no ma around, looks like he's stuck there with them two wild younguns to look after."

"Wonder where their mother is?" asked Scott.

I shook my head. "You saw how he clammed up when Willis asked him that."

Willis took a deep breath. "Well, I can state unequivocally that my mother would never leave me like that except in case of extreme emergency." I knew what he meant, but he should have left that big word in the dictionary.

When we got back to Balmy Springs, our

backpacks were lined up on a picnic table.

My legs felt shaky. "We've had company," I said.

Willis's hands went up in the air. "Oh, no," he moaned, "if someone stole my new camera, I'll, I'll . . ."

"You and me, too, if they took my binoculars," Scott added.

In a pinched second, we were going for our backpacks like ducks after June bugs.

5
Sticky Fingers on North Road

Willis was mighty relieved to find his expensive camera was okay. "I should have taken it with me," he declared. "Cameras are top items for thieves to lift. Guess I'm lucky."

Nothing was missing from Scott's backpack, either. His binoculars were right where he always kept them.

My pack just had junky stuff like a spool of fish line, hooks, corks, and pliers. And Ma's brownies.

Scott watched me lift out the plastic bag. When he saw it was zipped tight and flat empty, his nice, happy face turned gray with despair.

A little smile sneaked over Willis's round face. "It must have been the little people."

"Little people, my foot," I growled. "If you mean little Beans with sticky fingers, you got it, bubba. You're just plain lucky they didn't make off with your camera and Scott's binoculars."

Scott heaved a big sigh. "I knew we should have eaten those brownies before we left."

"Don't fret yourself," I told him. "I'll ask Ma to make some more for you. How 'bout we go cool off in the spring pool?"

We were soon splashing and making such a racket, we didn't hear Miz Lizzie West's tree-green pickup roll to a stop nearby. Her nephew, Biltmore, was driving, and helped her down from the truck.

Biltmore grins all the time. Pa says it's because Biltmore does not know any other way to stretch his head muscles. Ma called Pa's hand on that. She said it was plain that Biltmore used every scrap of brain the good Lord gave him. "Lizzie would be in a fix without him to do all that heavy work on the tree farm," she told Pa.

Biltmore is about thirty, but I reckon he weighs ten times that much. He's real cheerful and easy to get along with. I don't think he's got a mean bone in his big body. His favorite thing, when he can get away from Miz Lizzie, is treasure hunting. He likes shiny gum wrappers, rings from soft-drink cans, bird feathers, and such. He hides it from Miz Lizzie. She'd make him trash the junky stuff if he didn't.

Miz Lizzie had a real friendly-like howdy for us. "We come to get some healing water," she said. Biltmore was lifting jugs from the truck bed.

I introduced Scott and Willis to the two of them, then said, "We'll help you, Biltmore."

"Yeh-yah!" For Biltmore, that meant thank you or anything on the yes side of conversation.

34

"You're all such nice boys," Miz Lizzie said as we set the last jug in the truck bed. "Just be sure you don't fall in with bad company around here. There's a strange family a'living at Corn Kelly's place." She sniffed and lifted what little chin she had. "Judging from their dark features, they most likely come from Gypsy stock. That means they ain't to be trusted, Johnny. Gypsies steal things."

"For true?" The Beans had not looked like Gypsies to me, but what did I know?

"For true." She clasped her hands together, "Just don't know what the world's comin' to when people steal from the Lord's house. And they stole my yard tools from the shed." She sighed heavy-like. "You can't expect no good from people a'living in a school bus. A decent family'd build a home."

Scott said, "They're buil—"

"Well, maybe they're gonna build one," I cut in.

"It's so sad to see such people moving up here. But some of the workmen are all right. The nicest young black man asked to use my phone, offered to pay me, mind you. Course, I wouldn't let him, being it was a local call. It truly warms my heart to see a young person do right. Ain't enough like that anymore." She sighed and lifted her eyes toward heaven. "May the Lord preserve this healing water from evildoin' strangers!"

"Yes'm, amen." That seemed the proper thing for me to say.

She waddled back to the truck and waited for Biltmore to help her climb back in. "I 'spect we best get this fresh water home," she said to me. "We still got to go down to your Uncle Elbert's highway store for groceries."

Before Biltmore cranked up the truck, Miz Lizzie poked her head out the window. "Just you and your nice friends stay away from them Beans, Johnny. The Bible says we ain't to cast our pearls before swine, you know."

As the pickup rolled out of sight, Scott shook his head. "Johnny, she called the Beans swine. That's pigs."

"Uh-huh. But I'd be going back on my raising if I showed disrespect to Miz Lizzie. Pa says her nose never has laid down proper. He says we got to overlook how she brags 'bout her great-grandpa once owning one of the biggest plantations in the low country."

"No kidding? What happened to it?"

"Sherman's men burned it during the Civil War. All they had left was the silver they hid and the house up here. Miz Lizzie still calls it her summer home. Shucks, it's all the home she ever knew."

I hunched up my shoulders. "Ma says she's due credit for turning that place into a Christmas tree farm to support herself."

"But don't you think God wants us to speak up when we hear somebody put down other people?"

Scott had a bit of a frown on his face.

I studied on that for a dead minute. "Well, it ain—isn't like I couldn't. But first, I'd just have to be sure the Lord gave me the right way to say it." I didn't see any call to mention how I tended to shoot off my mouth before asking the Lord or anybody else.

"My mother likes for me to be nice to old people," said Willis. "And how can we be sure the Beans aren't thieves? Their place is the nearest one to the church, and those twins are pretty wild."

"All I know is they ate our brownies." Scott picked up a rock, turned it over, then flipped it away. "But then again, I guess little kids snitching brownies isn't exactly stealing. Who hasn't raided the fridge?"

"Count out Scott Jenkins," I said with a chuckle.

Scott checked his watch. "It's time to be starting back to your house, isn't it?"

My clock is in my head. "I'd say we got just enough time to stop by the church first, if it's okay with you guys."

It was.

A few minutes later, we stood before a new sign that said LOG CHAPEL. Everything else at the church looked the same, but a tan-colored Plymouth, old and faded, was parked out front. I didn't remember ever seeing the strange car before.

"Maybe the Jimson University guys are still staying here," Scott said. "Dad said they came back

37

this summer, trying to save trees."

I brushed the hair from my wet forehead and wiped it with the back of my hand. "Pa said Hank and Rusty left more'n two weeks ago, before the sound system got stolen. He also said Sandy McRee didn't plan to move back here till time to haul us to school again."

"Then who could it be?" Scott wanted to know.

"We'll find out soon enough." I clamped my lips together in a tight line like all my scared feelings might jump out of my mouth. Had the thieves come back? I wanted to say, "Let's forget stopping here now. Let's just run for that old log and get across the creek to safety."

But I didn't. I figured that if God wasn't in His own house, He wasn't anywhere. I breathed deep and knocked on the door.

6
Church Puzzles

"Sandy, it's you!" I was never so happy to see our preacher, or so glad to hug him. He had stayed in the dorm at Cougarville College all summer because he was in a hurry to get into a seminary.

Sandy stood back and looked at me. "You're taller, Johnny."

"Just a mite. I reckon it's time. You know Scott and Willis?"

He said he sure did, and invited us inside. But soon as we got through the door, the puzzled look on his face got my attention.

"Guess you heard about our new sound system disappearing, Johnny." He clasped his big hands and moved them up and down.

"Yep. Pa told me what a shock it was to find it missing when he got here last Sunday."

"I think I hate it most for his sake," said Sandy. "Your pa wanted it to be a surprise for you and Louise when you came back from the island."

"Has the sheriff been up to see about it?"

"Oh, yes, but he said it was happening all over,

and if they could solve one theft, then they might get to the bottom of most of the others."

"We did okay without a sound system," I said. "I reckon the Lord's got His hand on it."

Sandy smiled. "Good thinking, Johnny. Maybe we ought to stop and pray."

We all held hands and agreed that God was in charge of where that sound system would end up. Sandy says when you go asking the Lord for something, it's best to just turn it over to Him. He says details that wear people out don't amount to half of nothing to God. And you don't have to go looking for the Lord when you need His help, because He's always right there.

After the prayer, we checked all the doors and windows. They were locked. A new glass had been put in one of them.

"That's where the thief broke it and undid the latch," Sandy said. "Then he must have left by the door."

"Could the thief be someone in the church?" asked Scott.

Sandy shook his head. "I can't think of any of our folks doing something like this."

"How about the Jimson University guys who were staying here?" asked Willis.

"Hank and Rusty wouldn't steal," I snapped, "and they left before the system was put in."

Willis said, "Maybe it was the Bea—"

"Beatles!" Scott laughed as he elbowed Willis to shush him, for which I was glad. Sandy would hear Miz Lizzie's "Bean story" soon enough.

Sandy sighed. "I'm glad the men put up an outside light. Since I have a car now, I might as well move back up here Sunday morning."

"You mean that old car out there?" No sooner was that comment out of my mouth than I knew I should not have said it. Old Blue, our station wagon, looks like it belongs to Pa. But that pitiful vehicle sitting out front didn't come near to being what I thought our cool-looking preacher ought to drive.

Sandy grinned. "That old car got me up here without a hitch, Johnny. If I move in now, we'll have some time to get you ahead in your reading before school starts."

"Reckon I can live with that." Later, I'd tell him I was reading through the Bible on my own. Not only had Sandy driven us to school last year, but he also tutored us so we could catch up on school work we'd missed.

"Stop by for me Sunday, and I'll help you move."

"Offer accepted, Johnny."

After Sandy left, we walked the creek log and headed on the path through the woods to my house.

"Fellow Hermiteers," said Willis, "we have a mystery on our hands."

"And more than one incident," Scott added.

"Naw," I put in, "stealing yard tools or brownies ain't nothing much."

"My dad said our church's sound system cost a thousand dollars." Scott checked his watch. "Jeepers! Mom's probably waiting for us now."

We made quick plans to camp out overnight at the hut in a day or two and hunt for clues. Then we hurried to my house.

Before I went to sleep that night, I thought about the strangers we met that day, especially the Beans. Maybe they were thieves like Miz Lizzie said. Then again, maybe not. I just wished Wylie had told us his mother's whereabouts.

Strangers sure can act strange.

7
Beans for Supper

Two days later, about mid-afternoon, we set up camp in front of the hermit hut.

First off, we all had a drink of water from the cooler I brought along.

It was my idea for us to put our sleeping bags near the campfire on the ledge. "If it rains, the hut's right there. If it don't, we can count stars to go to sleep tonight."

We decided we ought to eat while we still had plenty of light. We made a fire and dragged out the big box from inside the hut. On it went buns, wieners, and containers of ketchup, mustard, and relish.

After whittling sharp edges on sticks, we waited for the coals to redden. Afternoon shadows crisscrossed the slope, and a little bitty breeze was stirring.

Being there with my friends was too good for me to go and get that creepy feeling of being watched all over again, but this time it was stronger than before. Maybe I ought to mention it to the other guys, after all. "Scott, I feel like—"

"Hey, the fire looks just right," Scott broke in to say. "Let's cook our supper." He pierced a plump wiener with the sharp end of a stick and held it over the red embers. Soon the air was filled with the mouth-watering smell and the popping sizzle of toasted meat.

The only way we ever kept Midnight away from a cookout was by locking him in Aunt Lou's barn. With perfect timing, the big dog bounded from behind a rock and near about knocked me down.

"Watch it!" I hollered, then went back to making my first hot dog.

In the next second, I saw two little heads pop out from behind Midnight's hiding rock, then duck back out of sight.

"Okay, Coyt and Callie!" I called out, not looking up. "You might's well come on out. I saw you."

Midnight ran behind the rock, then came back, nudging the twins ahead of him. "Mother Midnight!" I jeered. "Old dog, you done took on more trouble than a one-eyed cat with three mice to watch. Why dump it on us?"

Willis and I traded disgusted looks, but welcome was spread all over Scott's smiling face. The twins edged a bit closer, their big eyes looking like moonlit pools.

Somebody had to be tough. "Is Wylie with you?" I asked sharply.

"He's home," they said together.

"You don't belong up here by yourselves." I sounded mean.

"What'll you two have on your hot dogs?" Scott was no help at all. Coyt was at his elbow in a flash. "Everything!" he sang out.

Callie's big eyes went from Willis to me. I was about to squeeze mustard on my hot dog when her loud "STOP!" made me halt.

"Don't want no mustard on mine," she yelled. Plainly, I had no choice but to hold mustard and anything else she didn't want on a hot dog that was no longer mine.

I tossed a wiener to sad-eyed Midnight, who caught it in mid-air and hauled it into the bushes.

By the time Scott and I loaded two wieners on each stick for toasting, the twins were ready for seconds.

"I can cook my own hot dog," Callie said, but I held onto the stick as her little arm reached for it.

"Where'd you get that ugly scrape on your arm, Callie?" I asked.

Having his mouth full didn't stop Coyt from cutting in. "On a rock. I told her not to climb it, but she don't listen. Girls can't climb worth nothing. Just boys are strong."

"Shut up," Callie told him, reaching over to give her brother a quick shove. As she did, she lost her balance, and plunged headlong toward the fire. I dropped my stick and grabbed her as quick as I could, but not before the arm that wasn't scraped connected with the red coals.

Callie's screams were loud and awful. She tried to kick herself away from me, but I held on to her.

For a split second, I felt homesick for the time when there was just me and Midnight tromping all over the mountain, gathering Aunt Lou's herbs. I was about fed up with Beans—with Wylie for not keeping his brother and sister at home, with Mr. Bean for putting so much on Wylie.

But I had just part of a teeny second for that to run past me. The burn looked real bad, and I was scared Callie might go into shock.

When Willis came over with his first aid kit, her screaming got even worse. I told him to fetch my windbreaker from my sleeping bag. I put it around her.

"I think the best thing is for us to get her to my Aunt Lou's," I said.

Midnight came out of the bushes, sopping wet. He shook himself, and Coyt went over to hug him.

I frowned at the dog. "Where'd you get so wet so fast?" I said. "You couldn't have gone to the creek and back."

"He didn't have to," piped Coyt, cocking his chin to one side. "There's water coming out of a rock over there." He pointed to the right of where Hermit Dan's stone steps went down to the next ledge. "C'mon, Scott. I'll show you."

46

The two of them were gone before I could stop them. "Then hurry," I yelled after them.

At the foot of the stone steps, they turned to the right, pushed through leafy bushes, and out of sight.

"It's a little spring coming out of the rocks!" Scott yelled back.

"So Hermit Dan *did* have water close by," Willis said.

I wanted to go and see for myself, but a little moan from Callie held me back. "Shake a leg," I called to the others. "We got to get this youngun to Aunt Lou."

8
Aunt Lou's Healing

We pocketed our flashlights, which we were sure to need before we got back. Up on Mirror Mountain, it's like God pulls a big switch to turn off the daylight. One minute the sun's hanging low, the next it's gone.

We took Top Trail to Mirror Rock, then headed down Mirror Rock Road.

When we got to the North Road fork-off, Willis said, "Shouldn't Wylie know about this?"

"I reckon so," I said. I put Callie on Scott's strong shoulders. "You get her on to Aunt Lou, and I'll fetch Wylie."

When I passed the construction site on my way, men were still working. Good. I wasn't hankering to face more than one Bean just then.

Wylie must have seen me coming. He came out of the shadowy old shack to meet me, looking at me like I was a pest.

He went pale when I told him what had happened. "Gee whiz! I let time get away from me. I shoulda known it was too quiet."

He didn't want to face his dad right then, so he left a note and we cut through the woods to Aunt Lou's.

When we got to her porch, Louise was reading a Bible story to the twins.

Callie held up both bandaged arms to Wylie. "Aunt Lou blew the fire from my arm," she said proudly. "Then she put on cream to cool it."

"Aunt Lou's a magician," Coyt announced.

"I told you wasn't no magic to it. All I did was trust the Lord and anoint the burn with my wild herb cream. You can take some of my cream for when you change bandages. But keep 'em loose so the burn can get air."

Soon, we were all washing down Aunt Lou's homemade cookies with blackberry punch. Scott, Willis, and I sat on the steps with ours, and Midnight begged. "Don't even think of it!" I told the dog.

Next I knew, Aunt Lou was asking Wylie to bring the twins to Sunday school. "Mr. Beans' more'n welcome too," she said.

Say what? I crossed my eyes at Scott and Willis. Knowing Miz Lizzie, she had already run down the Beans to the congregation, including Aunt Lou. But my great aunt is one bullheaded Finlay, for sure.

"W-we used to go to church when we lived in North Carolina," Wylie was telling her. "But right now, Sunday's the only time Dad has for us to get our kiln built. Maybe we can come later on."

Aunt Lou wasn't giving up. "We can fetch and get the twins home."

"But I need a pretty dress," Callie cut in.

"Hush," Wylie told her, looking embarrassed. "The truth is, those two have grown out of most of their clothes this summer. Dad says we've got to buy new ones before school starts."

Aunt Lou turned to Louise. "Well, now ain't that something? You been begging me to let you sew up something pretty from that new stack of piece goods we got."

"I sure have," agreed Louise, cutting her eye at Wylie.

"Oh, no," he objected. "Dad wouldn't want us to put you out that way." He was looking at my sister and blushing. Their eyes locked like both of them plumb forgot anybody else was there.

"I'd love to make outfits for Callie and Coyt." Louise's voice was leaking honey worse than a bee tree. "Please let me try," she cooed, "just to see if I can."

I knew he was a goner, but Wylie's smile was good to see. When they left, he promised to bring the twins back the next day if it was okay with Mr. Bean.

Scott, Willis, and I stayed to feed Aunt Lou's chickens. It was dark when we hit the road again, so we were glad for our flashlights.

When we turned onto North Road, it hit me that we ought to check by the church again before we headed back up the mountain. Scott and Willis both agreed.

We were soon walking past the construction site, which was lit up like a used car lot.

Loud country music blasted from the trailer marked OFFICE. A dirty white pickup sat near the door. Through the window, we could see the shadow of someone's head against the light.

"Must be the night watchman," Scott said.

"We ought to stop and ask him if he saw or heard anybody going toward the church last week," Willis suggested.

We knocked, but we had to beat on the door before the man turned down the music and opened it.

"Yeah? Wha'ya want?" The outside lights lit up a bulldog face and bushy hair that looked like coiled snakes. He glared at us through cigarette smoke that was mixed with the smell of beer. His eyes looked suspicious as a hungry cat's.

9
Wonderings to Sleep On

"What you younguns doing 'round here this time of night?" There was a growl in the man's voice.

I stepped forward. "I'm Johnny Finlay, and this here's my two friends, Scott Jenkins and Willis Thompson." I put out my hand, but he didn't shake it.

"We're camping on the mountain," explained Scott. "You must be the night watchman, Mister, er . . ."

"Hale. And you got it right. With all the equipment out there, s'my job to see Byall ain't stole blind."

We backed off from a gust of his second-hand smoke.

"Smoking's bad for your health," warned Willis.

"So they tell me. Something else that ain't too healthy is for you boys to be prowling 'round other people's property at night."

"Mr. Hale, we wasn't prowling," I spoke up. "We saw your light and—" I fanned smoke from my face.

Who did this man think he was, talking to me like that on my own mountain?

Scott picked up where I left off. "We just wondered if you might've noticed anybody going into the church driveway at night. Lately, that is."

"Somebody lifted the chapel's sound system," said Willis. "Amplifiers, mikes, everything."

"You don't say? Well, that's too bad," the big man rasped. "But I can't see that driveway from here at night. Look for yourself."

We did. The glow from the outside lights turned into fog as it rode the mist from the creek.

"Can't see nothing past the creek, sir."

"Me neither. You boys the onliest ones I seen, 'cept for . . ." he scratched his head, "that big fella from the tree farm down the road."

"Biltmore?"

"That's it." He took another slurp of beer from the can. "Acts like his bread—cough, cough—never quite got done."

"Biltmore's always walking 'round the mountain when Miz Lizzie can't think of work she wants him to do," I explained.

"To say he lopes'd be more like it. I told him to stay away from here. Too many tools for him to pick up. Same goes for you boys." He coughed again. "Anyhow, I ain't paid to keep an eye on that church. You sure you boys wasn't the ones who done it?"

That got my dander up, but I didn't hanker to pick a patch of peas I couldn't shell. The man was twice my size. We thanked him and moved on.

The outdoor light was shining at the Log Chapel. Finding no signs of another break-in, we took a path to Top Trail.

Back at the ledge in front of the hermit hut, we built up the fire and toasted more wieners. This time, we got to eat our hot dogs in peace.

"Do you think it was Biltmore?" Willis asked.

I shook my head. "Biltmore picks up bits of trash, but he ain't mean or smart enough to steal less'n somebody put him up to it."

"Not the Beans, I hope." said Willis.

I shrugged. "If Bilt's got that cozy with 'em, I'll guarantee you, Miz Lizzie don't know it."

Scott finished his hot dog and looked at the red coals. "Even so, I can't see the Beans as thieves."

"What about that night watchman?" asked Willis. "He could have gone and loaded that sound system in his pickup one night and covered it up and hauled it off the next morning."

"And if asked, he could pin it on Biltmore," I said. "Hale might bear watching."

"We need proof and a motive," Willis said.

"Motive's easy," said Scott. "Booze and cigarette money."

Willis yawned. "Let's sleep on it."

Soon we were in our sleeping bags. It was a clear

night, and the stars winked down at us.

I was the last to go to sleep because I couldn't get the Beans off my mind. I wanted to trust Wylie, but he was like two different people. One minute he was nice; the next, uptight.

Mirror Mountain has been home to us Finlays for nigh on to two hundred years. I reckon we're just hard put to try and figure out people who don't think like us or treasure all the wild things that live up here. Lying there, with sounds of night critters stroking the cool air, I didn't ever want to have to fall asleep to any other noise.

"Help me know who to trust," I prayed. "It ain't easy with all these strangers coming to my mountain."

It wasn't out loud, but what God said was plain as day inside my head. He said, "It's not your mountain, Johnny Elbert."

10
The Gleam of Silver

Midnight was there at daybreak, licking my face. I sat up, and he sat back, smiling.

"I reckon you're powerful pleased with yourself," I said, trying to keep my voice down. But the dog took it on himself to talk back with a sharp yip, which woke up Scott and Willis.

I had put a slow-burning log on the fire during the night. Over the still-hot coals, we toasted thick hunks of Aunt Lou's sourdough bread, and dunked it in Pa's sourwood honey.

"Call our breakfast sweet and sour," Scott quipped, washing it down with cold chocolate milk. I don't know why he doesn't get fat. Maybe he only eats like that when he's around me.

After breakfast, Midnight went with me to see the spring. When we came back, Willis was tickled pink to get a shot of the wet dog shaking himself against the sunrise.

We took our own sweet time cleaning up and

storing our stuff inside the hut. Then we took off on a hike to see the houses Byall was having built down North Road.

Right after we passed Miz Lizzie's house, we walked across Second North Bridge. In the thick woods ahead of us, we heard the whir of power saws and the bamming of loud hammers.

Closer to us, a whangy sound took over. Someone was playing a harmonica. In between the WHANNH WHANNH notes, that person was singing. We stopped to listen.

(WHANNH)
I come up on this mountain
Wearin' name-brand shoes;
Now I'm here just a'singin'
Mirror Mountain blues, oh yeah.
(WHANNH WHANNH WHANNH WHANNH)

Got them blues on the mountain,
Mirror Mountain blues. . . .
(WHAN-NH WHANNH)
Rather be with my beh-BEEEH
Down in Saint Matthews.
(WHAN-NY WHAN-NY WHAN-NY)
Mirror Mountain blue-HOOOH-OOH-S.

Around the next curve, a young black man with humongous shoulders sat in the open back door of a dark gray van. Like one of the Atlanta Braves, he wore his hair flattop-box style, and name-brand shoes.

"How do," he said, flashing a real friendly smile. "Name's Tyrell. Where you headin'?"

We told him our names and how we wanted to see what was being built further down the road.

"Ahll right!" he said, looking at his watch, which looked like it cost plenty. "I'm one of the carpenters, and my break time's starting to run out. I'll walk along with you."

He popped his harmonica against his jeans, and pocketed it. Before locking the van, he got a workman's hard hat from it. "Got to lock up good these days," he said.

"Neat van," Scott told him.

"Did you compose the song you were singing?" Willis wanted to know.

"You got it. One of these days, I'm hopin' to make it to Nashville—or Hollywood, might be."

"I was at Wistero Island this summer," I told him. "It's not far from Saint Matthews. That your home?"

Tyrell threw back his head and laughed all the way to his shiny-buckled belt. "Man, I ain't never even been to Saint Matthews. It was just the onliest town on the South Carolina map that rhymed with blues."

We laughed with him.

Tyrell waved to the workmen as we passed the cottages that were going up. The men waved back at him. He pointed out short, red-flagged stobs that marked off lots where more houses would go up later.

"I don't see why you can't fit them houses in there without cutting down so many trees," I muttered.

"Ain't it so? We try to leave as many as we can."

"I'd love to live in a house up here," said Scott.

Willis nodded. "Me too. That way the Hermiteers could get together most anytime."

I let my mind taste how it might be to have my friends living nearby. It would take some getting used to.

After Tyrell went back to work, we headed back up the road.

"What a nice guy—Tyrell," Scott said.

Willis nodded, "Even if his blues are corny."

"Well, I reckon he's about the friendliest of all the Byall crew we've run into yet," I agreed.

We stopped for a drink at Balmy Springs and found Coyt and Callie patting out mud pies on a table. They were covered with mud. Callie's arm bandages looked downright nasty. Coyt's short jeans were about to fall off. A closer look told me it was because of a flashlight in his back pocket that pulled them below his waist.

Midnight bounded over to them for a hug, then jumped into the pool. The twins giggled as they watched him.

I caught myself a dipper of water. "You younguns aiming to set up a playhouse here?" I asked.

Callie went over to the gully under the drainage hole and dipped up a big spoonful of wet mud. "We got lots of playhouses," she said, "like the one you was camping at, and this one." Her great big eyes opened wider. "And one's got hidden trea—b-but that un's a secret." She cut her eye at her brother.

"Motor Mouth!" Coyt shouted at his sister.

"Am not! I didn't tell 'em where, Mr. Know-it-all."

She wound up and pitched a spoonful of mud at her brother. He dodged, then tried to yank the big spoon from her.

"Hold it there," I yelled. Coyt let go, and the spoon was like a mirror as a ray of bright sunshine lit it up.

"Where'd you get that spoon, Callie?" I asked.

"She found it in the woods," Coyt cut in.

"Let me look at it," said Willis, reaching toward her.

Callie backed off, and Willis's face made a prefect target for Coyt's handful of mud.

"Hey, that's not nice!" yelled Willis, looking so shocked, it was hard not to laugh at him as he washed his glasses in the pool.

"Did you find that flashlight too?" I asked.

Coyt held on to the flashlight as he hitched up his shorts. "It's mine!" he bellowed.

I squinted over Callie's shoulder. "That looks like the spoon Miz Lizzie brings to church picnics."

"Mean old woman," Callie muttered. "Always telling us to go home."

"Maybe it is Miz Lizzie's spoon," Scott suggested.

"Naw," I decided, "hers has a big W on it, for West. This one's plain."

"It's real silver, though," Scott noticed.

Callie's grip on that spoon didn't let up one bit. "It's my mixing spoon," she insisted.

"But it's too nice for mud pies," Scott told her. "You should put it back wherever you got it."

"Nohhh!" screeched Coyt. "We didn't steal that spoon. We found it."

"You want to tell us where?" Willis asked. "And was it the only shiny treasure you found?"

Callie started to shake her head, but Coyt elbowed her real fast. She dropped her big brown eyes toward the mud pie, smoothing and patting it with the back of the shiny spoon.

Coyt stuck out his bottom lip. "You guys stop buggin' us," he snapped, making it plain that quiz time was over.

"Okay, we'll let you be," I said, "but try not to scratch up that nice spoon." As we turned to head out, I gave the twins a sideways look. "But if it was me, I'd feel mighty rotten keeping something I knew wasn't mine."

"We gonna put it back where we found it!" Coyt yelled after us as we walked away. "But that's for just me and Callie to know, Johnny Finlay."

"All right. But I hope you don't fall off any more rocks or into any more fires while you're tromping all over creation by yourselves."

11
Treetop Lookout

Back on the road, I turned to Scott. "How much time we got till your folks come?" I had a fair idea myself, just from noticing where the sun was. But his watch is an expensive one, and I thought he ought to get his money's worth.

"We still got a couple hours," he said, "allowing time to go back to the hut for our sleeping bags and coolers."

"Well, this oughtn't take more'n an hour. I don't know this side of the mountain too good, but I know we can get to the woods back of the Bean place by walking alongside Miz Lizzie's tree farm."

"Why do we need to go there?" asked Willis.

"Remember what Callie let slip about hidden treasure in a secret playhouse? I got a hunch it's somewhere back there."

"Do you think Wylie knows about it, Johnny?" Scott asked.

"Beats me. Till we find out more, we won't tell him nothing."

"What if Miz Lizzie threw that one spoon out with

63

her garbage," Willis suggested. "I mean, unintentionally, like my grandmother does. She's always getting me to slosh through those smelly bags to find something that's missing."

"That might be," Scott said, "but I'm for making a good search, to be sure."

I led the way down the edge of Miz Lizzie's tree farm. It stopped at a line of high bald rocks. After getting there, we made a left turn.

"Them high rocks go all the way across to Spin Rock on Mirror Rock Road," I told the boys. "Watch for snakes."

Saying that put me to worry a mite about the twins running wild like they did. After they showed up at the hermit hut, there was no telling where else they had been.

We found no sign of a place where a thief might hide his loot. Not in the woods, nor along the line of tall rocks.

"We're wasting time," I said. "I think I'll climb that tall sycamore over there. I want to see what's on the other side of them high rocks."

"Take my binoculars," Scott offered.

I strapped them around my neck, then hugged the tree trunk. Frog-fashion, I crept to the highest limb that tested strong. In the crook of it, I settled myself and looked through the binoculars.

"What do you see?" Scott hollered from below.

"Right now, I'm looking back where we been," I

yelled down to them. "Miz Lizzie's Christmas tree farm looks like a big patchwork quilt. Willis, you shoulda tied your camera onto me too."

"Maybe so, but what's over the rocks?" Willis asked.

I shifted the binoculars to my left. "More rocks," I yelled, "and a great big one with the road going round it . . . hey, that's Spin Rock! And there's Way High Creek a'curling down the mountainside. I can see the bridge where Mirror Rock Road crosses it. Yep, I oughta have the camera up here with me." I thought I heard Willis groan.

About that time, I caught my breath as something else showed up in my line of vision. "Well, I declare!" I croaked.

"What—what—what?" Scott's voice was impatient.

"It's . . . er . . . one of them big-sized campers settin' by the creek."

"Fishermen, maybe?"

"Maybe. I'm coming down now." I made short work of getting my feet back on the ground.

"Couldn't you see anything else?" Scott asked.

I shook my head. "Too many trees around it. Must be nigh on to 500 feet of thick woods from that camper to the bridge on Mirror Rock Road. It's a puzzle how anybody drove it in."

"Let's go investigate," said Willis. "I might get some shots that could be used for evidence later."

I eyed the high rocks and shook away a piece of hay-brown hair from my forehead. "Naw, not today. Except for where the creek cuts through, there's nothing but solid high rocks all the way to Spin Rock." I gave the binoculars back to Scott. "That camper had to get off Mirror Rock Road somewhere below the bridge. We'd have to go in that way too, and we 'bout run out of time today."

We did, in fact, have to shake a leg to pick up our stuff at the hut and get back to my house.

Mrs. Jenkins was already there on the back porch, drinking iced tea and going through a tray of Ma's painted Scripture rocks. After she paid for the ones she wanted, she herded her passengers into their blue van.

Scott and Willis talked to me from their seats at the open back window. "We'll see if we can find where the camper got off Mirror Rock Road," Scott said in a low voice.

"Get your heads inside, boys," called Mrs. Jenkins. "I'm closing that window."

"Please, Mom, not till we cross the creek," begged Scott. "We'll fasten our seat belts."

Mrs. Jenkins said that sounded fair enough.

"Don't forget to look," I hollered to Scott and Willis as they drove off.

"Look for what?" asked my nosy sister, who had just come outside.

I fixed her with a silly face, then ducked and

scooted inside to wash up for dinner.

Later, Scott phoned back to say there were tire tracks leaving the road "right after we crossed the bridge. Bet it was Hale's pickup. When can we go and check?" He sounded excited.

"Ummmmh. Let me study on it a couple days and get back to you." I wasn't sure what step I would take next, but even before we hung up, I knew it wouldn't be safe enough for ten year olds to tag along.

Aunt Lou says when we don't know what we're up against, the Bible says we're to be smart like snakes and gentle like doves. It's in the tenth chapter of Matthew.

I know, because I looked it up.

12
Holy Chaos

Sunday morning, when Sandy stopped to pick me up, he smelled breakfast cooking. He agreed with Ma that we had time for a breakfast of steaming grits topped with ham and red-eye gravy.

Any one of us Finlays would do just about anything for Sandy McRee. Aunt Lou always said our help would come from the Lord. After hearing Sandy preach, Pa quit moonshining and we all got born anew.

After breakfast, I crawled into Sandy's car. A suck-egg hound would not have been proud to ride in that crummy flivver, but it got us to the church without a hitch.

We found the whole place neat and clean.

"Miz Lizzie and Biltmore must have come yesterday," said Sandy.

"Anybody 'sides them got a key?"

"Just your Uncle Elbert."

In no time, we had that ugly car unloaded. Then Sandy showered and dressed to go say howdy to early comers out front.

I stayed inside to ponder things for a minute. Biltmore again. Had he sneaked the key from his aunt? But if he had, how could he have hidden a whole sound system from Miz Lizzie? And what use would he have for one away from the church? He was no musician. Biltmore couldn't even carry a tune.

I could have done without a shower, but I went on and took a quick one, then changed into my clean clothes.

Sandy's bedroom window looked down through pines to Way High Creek. I could hear it gurgling over rocks. Birds sang in the trees and shrubbery. I watched a bright-colored hummingbird tasting pink abelia blooms. Then I heard a car motor wind down out front.

Miz Lizzie's tree-green pickup was out front, and she had poor Sandy backed into a corner of the porch, bending his ear with her sorrows.

Biltmore stood nearby, so I went and stood by him, trying to hear what Miz Lizzie was saying.

"How you doing, Bilt," I said.

"Fine, Johnny. Yeh-yah, fine," he said with his usual big smile. Biltmore is always fine.

". . . Thursday, when we come home with groceries," sobbed Miz Lizzie, "back door glass was broke, same's here."

Sandy was writing in a little notebook. "Now I've got silver—pitcher, platter, table pieces. And did you say two big serving spoons and your Civil War rifle?"

Miz Lizzie's hands went up desperate-like. "All gone."

Sandy sighed. "Did you call the sheriff?"

"I did, and told him 'bout the Beans, and my yard tools a'missing. He acted like them tools wasn't worth his time. Why, poor Biltmore ain't been able to clean the yard all week for needing 'em."

All the time Miz Lizzie talked, Biltmore pulled at his necktie, which always lands in his pocket before church is over. Now I noticed him looking down at his size 14 shoes, not smiling. *He knows something*, I thought. Maybe I ought to flat out ask him, but I couldn't figure a way to go about it.

"There, there," Sandy's voice was soft and caring. "We'll do all we can to help you get your things back."

Miz Lizzie straightened her hefty self up. "Best thing'd be to run that man and his wild younguns off the mountain."

Pa and Uncle Elbert drove up about the same time, so I left Biltmore to go help unload all the guitars and picnic food from the two cars.

Ray Arthur, my redheaded cousin, had already heard about Miz Lizzie's robbery. "Reckon she bragged about her valuables to one person too many." Then he crossed his chest like Miz Lizzie was doing and said, "Ohhhhh, what a terr'ble cross to bear." I had to laugh at him.

"Church ain't gonna be boring today," whispered Ray Arthur.

71

Church was never boring with Ray Arthur around. But Sandy's sermons didn't bore me either. One day soon, I aimed to ask my cousin if he ever felt eager to know the Lord better.

"Your family's grown," Ray Arthur noticed.

Louise stepped from the back door, then Aunt Lou. Next thing I saw was two dressed-up younguns. This time, there was no mistaking which was the boy and which was the girl.

Coyt Bean, wearing dark blue shorts and a red checked shirt, stood beside Aunt Lou, holding her hand. Callie was with Louise, who carried her guitar.

When the little girl saw me, she smiled all over her face. "We spent the night with Aunt Lou," she chirped. "Louise made me my dress." She spun around fast, and the skirt of her red checked dress whirled out in a circle around her. Long, puffy sleeves hid her bandages.

"Wow!" I said, "that's a lot of skirt."

Coyt frowned and pulled at his shirt collar. "Midnight's shut up in the barn."

Louise heard. "Coyt, I told you we'd let him out after the picnic. We have to go inside now."

Miz Lizzie was so caught up in sharing her bad news, she didn't see the twins till Aunt Lou said, "Mornin', Liz. Meet these special friends of mine— Coyt and Callie Bean."

Miz Lizzie's little thin-lipped mouth popped open, then clamped shut fast as a snapping turtle's. Her little parakeet nose sniffed air and held it till I thought she'd explode. Finally, she half nodded at the twins. Then it was time to go sing.

Pa and Louise got everybody clapping and singing "This Little Light of Mine." You could hear Biltmore above everybody else.

Miz Lizzie did not sing at all, just sat and glared at Aunt Lou like a cat that can't wait to pounce on a jaybird. I knew she was dying to get at her for bringing "swine" to church, but Aunt Lou was too busy praising the Lord to notice.

After praying for God to restore what was lost or stolen, Sandy preached from Hebrews 13:2. "Don't forget to be kind to strangers, for some who have done this have entertained angels without realizing it!"

I cut my eye from Miz Lizzie to the twins, who looked sweet as angels in their new clothes. I knew better. Sandy ought to explain that not ALL strangers were angels. Then I could feel a mite more saintly for wishing them off my mountain.

"Excuse me, Lord," I prayed. "I mean YOUR mountain. But You got lots of mountains in South Carolina. Why'd You let Will Byall pick ours to chop up?" I reared back in my seat and waited for the peace I always felt after praying. This time, it wasn't there.

Miz Lizzie didn't stay for the picnic after church, which wiped off Biltmore's smile in a hurry. I heard her say she didn't have the heart to serve her famous potato salad "without its usual serving spoon." I figured she meant the one with the W on it.

Coyt took a drumstick from every platter of fried chicken on the table. All told, he probably ate half the weight of a whole chicken.

Callie was too excited to eat much. She whirled around singing "Jesus Loves Me." Then she raised her hands and shouted, "Praise the Lord!"

"Amen!" said the people around her.

Right then, I just couldn't find it in me to bad-mouth the Beans, not even to myself. It wasn't that I was totally into trusting Wylie yet. And I had only seen his father that one time. I just wanted to prove Miz Lizzie was wrong about them.

That night, questions bounced up and down in my head, keeping me awake.

Were all of Miz Lizzie's stolen treasures in Callie's secret playhouse? Did Hale sleep at the camper during the day, and how well did he know the Beans? If Hale was the thief, were the Beans in with him on these robberies?

There was one hitch. There was no way for Coyt and Callie to reach that camper from their woods. The long line of boulders was too high. And far as I could tell, the creek was too fast and was apt to be real deep where it went under the rocks. Even the strongest swimmer would be a fool to try and swim under there to get to the other side.

Now I knew there were two things I needed to do. First, I had to look in the woods again. Second, I had to get to that camper and see who and what was in it.

I had to do it by myself. It was too big a risk for me to bring in Scott and Willis to help.

Something tightened inside me. "Just thinking about what could happen scares me silly, Lord," I prayed. "Please loan me some of Your courage, just enough to get me through what I gotta do."

13
The Man from Human Services

Monday morning I got up with a notion to go treasure hunting again and maybe check out that camper, but Pa's notion was for me to clean the yard before I headed anywhere. When Midnight came and saw me working, he took off by himself. A dog's life is sometimes better than a boy's.

With Pa at the store and Louise at Aunt Lou's, Ma and I were the only ones there for midday dinner. We had homemade vegetable soup and bread sticks Ma had cut and toasted from day-old bread.

It was newstime on the radio. The announcer reminded home owners to keep doors and windows locked at all times. "If you go on vacation, stop paper and mail deliveries," he went on, "and have a neighbor check your house daily."

Ma clicked off the little radio. "Sounds like there's lots more people being robbed than just Lizzie and the church."

"Ma, do you think she's right to accuse the Beans?"

"Son, you know how Miz Lizzie lets notions build up in her head. Your pa says no man who works all the time like Mr. Bean is likely to be out to get something for nothing."

I was glad to hear Ma say that, because I wanted to prove Miz Lizzie was wrong about the Beans.

After eating, I was out front weeding Ma's marigold bed when a yellow Olds Cutlass pulled into the yard and stopped. I could hardly see the driver behind the dark windows, but I knew right off that it was another meddling stranger. Mountain folks get out of the car the minute it halts.

The window by the driver's seat slid open. A long-faced black man peered at me through dark glasses. "Is this the Bean residence?" he asked.

"I—I reckon you missed your turn," I said. "I'm Johnny Elbert Finlay."

He had a skinny neck that stretched forward like a turtle's, making his Adam's apple stand out.

From the pocket of his white shirt, he drew out a picture ID card. I took my own sweet time reading, "Melvin Carroway, South Carolina Department of Human Services."

My chin went up a notch. "How do I know it's you in that picture, less'n you take off your glasses?"

His mouth flattened out to a straight line like I'd

insulted him, but he slid the glasses down to his nose.

Us Finlays don't take to being beholden to the U.S. Government. When Pa was sent up for moonshining, social workers came to sign us up for food stamps. Ma just said no, thank you, we would get on fine enough, which we did. You might say we went on eating high off the hog, thanks to Aunt Lou's garden, cow, and chickens.

After I agreed it was him in the picture, Mr. Carroway put back the ID and pushed up his glasses. "Can you direct me to the Beans' place, young man?"

I didn't hurry to answer. If I told him exactly how to get there, I might never know what he wanted with the Beans.

"I'll go show you, soon's I tell Ma."

Ma had been peeping at us from the window. She had already guessed he was from Human Services.

"If Lizzie ain't gone and sic'd the government on them poor Beans, I'll swallow a rock," she said. "Go with him, Johnny, but keep your head where your mouth is."

When I got back to his car, Mr. Carroway mashed a button to unlock the door from inside. I climbed into the front seat beside him, and we were on our way.

14
Casing the Caseworker

Melvin Carroway's Olds topped the hill in high gear and zoomed down the other side of the Beans' drive. He braked just before hitting the canvas shed.

Slowly, Mr. Carroway eased from his car. When he looked around, he stretched his neck way out from the rest of his lanky, loose-built body.

Just like before, Wylie hollered from inside the bus and shoved that old pipe out the window. When Melvin Carroway saw that, he stood there like a petrified cornstalk.

Maybe I should have told the man it wasn't a gun. Sometimes it seems like something bad gets ahold of me. Aunt Lou would probably name it, and most likely, she'd be right.

"P-please don't shoot, Mr. Bean," stammered Mr. Carroway. "I'm here for Hu-ooh-hu-man Services." He was waving his ID high in the air.

Just like before, the pipe was pulled back out of sight. When Wylie showed up at the door, I had to bite my lip to keep from laughing out loud.

Wylie folded his arms, and shot me a look that was cold as a well digger's toe. But the look he gave the man was about as sociable as you might expect from a mother wildcat. "We don't got business with Human Services," snapped Wylie.

"You look too young to be Potter Bean." Mr. Carroway pushed his sunshades down a tad and handed Wylie his ID.

Wylie looked at it, then at Melvin Carroway. "I'm Potter Bean's son," he told the man as he gave the card back to him. "I'm in charge here right now."

Mr. Carroway's bony fingers shook as he put back the ID and took out a little notebook. "You must be Wylie. Where are Coyt and Callie?"

Wylie unfolded his arms, and all the toughness seemed to go out of him. "They'rrre around . . . playing. Why?" It was plain to me that Wylie didn't have the faintest idea where the twins were.

The man raised his thick eyebrows. "Our office received a report of child neglect." He wiggled his mouth around like he was trying to loosen it up some. "It's my lawful duty to investigate within twenty-four hours." His voice sounded calmer.

Wylie looked around again before answering. "You gonna have to talk to my dad. He's laying stone at the construction site up the road there. I just look after things here while he's at work."

"Hmmm. That puts a lot of responsibility on a

young fellow like you. Do you ever hear from your mother?"

"Y-you ask Dad about that." Wylie stammered. "We're getting along just fine."

Carroway was still writing. His hand wasn't shaking now. "I'll go talk with your father, Wylie. But it would save a lot of time if I could see the children now. I need to document verification of their presence."

Wylie looked all around the clearing, then gave a loud whistle through his fingers.

From the myrtles at the top of the steep driveway, a big tractor tire quietly sped downhill toward us, with Midnight running beside it.

Mr. Carroway didn't see it. I've noticed that social workers tend to get so busy writing stuff down, they miss half of what's going on with folks they investigate.

I opened my mouth to warn him, but it was too late. The tire never wavered till, like a billy goat, it butted Melvin Carroway up and over. He landed on his backside, sprawled out like a spider. The notebook went one way, the pen another.

Out of the tire's inner circle bounced the twins, squealing for joy. Midnight's welcoming muddy paws were all over the man.

After I called off the dog, Callie pointed at Mr. Carroway. "Who's he?"

Wylie's face wore a satisfied smirk. "Y'all tell this

man from Human Services you're sorry."

The whoopla was over. Their wide eyes got even wider. "We sorry," they said together. Next thing I knew, Coyt was begging the man, "Please don't take us away. We won't run off from Wylie no more."

For the first time, I saw a really scared look in the children's eyes. They cowered next to Wylie, holding onto his T-shirt.

"I promise you nobody's taking you anywhere." Wylie put an arm around each of the twins.

Mr. Carroway opened his car door and sighed. "I'm ready to go," he said, "but I sure hate to muddy up my car seat."

Wylie sent the twins inside for newspapers to spread on the seat, and I fetched the man's pen and notebook for him.

Mr. Carroway turned to Coyt and Callie. "Don't worry," he said softly. "I don't take children from their folks unless I think they're in danger." A big grin split his long face. "From what I've seen up till now, it's other people who'd best be warned to keep their eyes open around you two."

After we were back in the car, Wylie shot a dirty look at me. "If you gotta talk to Dad," he said to the man, "I know Johnny'll be delighted to take you straight to him." His tone was downright sarcastic. I wished I could tell Wylie I was on his side, but the lid was already on the jar.

Mr. Carroway did want to talk to Mr. Bean, and he offered to take me home first. But I flat out wasn't going to miss hearing what those two men said to each other. "I'll hang around," I told him.

At the construction site, Sam Grove told Potter Bean he had more than one break coming to him. "Take all the time you need," he said.

When the two men gave me a sideways look, I made out like all my attention was on a concrete mixer churning mortar. After they got to talking, I snuck closer to listen.

Again, Mr. Carroway took out a pen and notebook.

"Child neglect, huh?" Mr. Bean said, "and did you find it like Miz West said you would?" He sounded annoyed.

"Mr. Bean, the source of my information must remain anonymous. What I did see was two little children who are a right big handful for a fifteen-year-old boy."

"The twins are active, all right, but they're healthier and happier now than they've ever been."

"True. But young children need a parent's discipline at home." Mr. Carroway tapped the notebook with his pen. "Your case history shows the judge gave you custody because their mother was declared incompetent. But when neighbors worry—"

"Neighbors-s-s? Why do you think I work so hard

here? I want to get my pottery going so I can be at home with my children."

"Well, I hope you're going to provide better shelter than that old school bus. And Wylie should not be pointing a gun at people. Guns around children . . ."

"A—a gun?" It was clear enough that Mr. Bean didn't know about Wylie's game with the fake firearm, so I butted in and told them all about it.

They looked surprised, but I could tell Potter Bean held back a snicker.

"Er-uh-well," stammered Carroway. "Johnny, this is private business, if you don't mind."

"Yes, sir," I said. "I'll just wait over by the car."

Under a tree near enough to hear the men, Boozer was smoking. When the talking was over, Sam Grove stuck his head out of the office and called Boozer to come see him.

Mr. Carroway offered to drive me home again, but I said, "Before you go down the mountain, I want you to meet my Aunt Lou."

"Can she tell me more about the Beans?"

"My Aunt Lou can tell you most anything you need to know," I said. "She doctored Callie's burn. She and my sister sewed up Sunday outfits so's to get them younguns to church." Just for insurance I added, "and they sometimes stay the night at Aunt Lou's." I didn't see any need to say they had only done that once.

15
A Good Word Is Said

After I introduced the stranger to her, Aunt Lou sent Louise to fetch a pitcher of chilled grape juice. "Come set a spell," she told him.

Mr. Carroway stated his business. He kept fidgeting in his chair, digging at the dry mud on his shirt.

"What else did Busy Lizzie tell you?" asked Aunt Lou.

"That she thought—Miz Finlay! I didn't say who called." He tried to brush beads of sweat from his M-shaped hairline.

"Didn't have to. Lizzie means well, but she blows her 'sumptions to high heaven. Let me tell you, Mr. Carry-away—"

"Cah-ROH-way, Ma'am."

"Whatever. Just write in that there book that there ain't no need for you to come traipsin' up here a'buggin' them Beans ever whipstitch. I'll call you if there's need."

"Aunt Lou don't never break a promise," I put in.

Melvin Carroway smiled, looking pleased. "Ma'am, I'm writing that as long as neighbors like you are around, the report of child neglect is unfounded."

He sipped the grape drink Louise poured for him. He said it was the most refreshing one he ever had, so Aunt Lou poured him another one.

As the yellow Olds disappeared down the road, Aunt Lou said, "Johnny, I'd be obliged if you'd feed my chickens. I got to pray for me 'fore I go and tell the Lord He ought to shut Lizzie's mouth for a spell."

Midnight came loping up to the barn while I shelled corn for the chickens.

"You sure you come to the right house?" I asked as he snaked toward me on his belly. "Wish you could tell me where that treasure's hid. Nahhh. Reckon you done turned to lovin' Coyt and Callie better'n you do me."

The dog rubbed against my knee, then sat and put his paw up for a handshake. "Maybe not," I said, hugging his neck.

When I got home, the TV was going full blast in the big front room. I don't usually take much notice of the news, but I did an about-face when I heard the man say Mirror Mountain.

16
Corn Shucking Time

There on the screen was a mug shot of big, bad Corn Kelly. In the front view, he snarled at the camera. The side view showed his flabby double chin, with the bushy beard shaved from it. "Kelly escaped early this morning," said the announcer. "If you see this man, please notify the Cougarville County Sheriff's Department. He is not considered to be dangerous, but you are advised to exercise extreme caution."

I gasped. "You hear that, Ma? MA? PA?" Nobody answered. I was home alone, and Corn Kelly was loose on the mountain. A cold chill ran over me.

I tore out the back door and covered the distance between me and Mirror Rock in two minutes flat. Like I figured, Ma and Pa were there watching the sunset and holding hands like they just found each other.

Pa's about half Corn's size, but he never was scared of him. He just hooted over the idea of "exercising caution."

"Son," he said, looking me straight in the eye, "Corn might be a no-good yellow coward, but he ain't got the nerve to lay a hand on a son of mine." He scratched the back of his ear. "It's just money he's after."

Then why was I trembling? Pa hugged my shoulder. "Son, I love you more'n I can say, but just bear in mind that God loves you even more. He's with you all the time I ain't. You don't have to be a'feared of no man."

I thought about that as we walked back home, but Ma wasn't for taking chances. She sent Pa to fetch Aunt Lou and Louise to our house. The minute he left, she put me to sliding chairs under doorknobs while she checked the latches on windows and closed the curtains.

Scott phoned and said he and Willis were mad because their parents had made the mountain off-limits till Corn was back behind bars. I told him I wasn't planning to risk running into Corn Kelly, either.

I had hardly hung up the phone when I was faced with having to change that very same plan.

17
Lost in the Night

While Ma and I waited for the others to get back, we stayed tuned to a Greenville TV station to hear more about Corn's escape. The TV said he hid in a laundry truck, and "based on reports of thefts on Mirror Mountain, authorities believe Kelly may be involved."

"I reckon Corn's out to do all the meanness he can," Ma said. "It'd be just like him to try and get back at the county fer taking his property." She stopped and looked at me. "You knocking on something, Johnny?"

"No, Ma'am." I felt like I couldn't breathe. "Someone's at the door," I said. It was too soon for Pa to be coming back. I eyed his gun on the wall.

"Leave that gun be!" Ma said as she turned off the inside light.

The knocking got louder. Ma pushed the curtain back a little for the two of us to see out.

In the glow of the outside light, I made out Potter Bean's scared face. With him was Sandy McRee, which was reason enough for Ma to open the door.

"Mrs. Finlay, this is Potter Bean," Sandy said. "The twins haven't come home. Wylie's checking at Aunt Lou's, and we wondered if they came here."

Ma shook her head. "Wish they had."

"Slipped off from Wylie just before I got home from work," explained Mr. Bean. "We hunted and called 'em all over the woods around our place. They didn't answer." He stopped to take a long, shaky breath.

"They might be at the hermit hut," I thought out loud.

"What hermit?" Potter Bean frowned.

"Oh, Hermit Dan's dead," I told him. "Me and my friends use his old hut for a clubhouse. That's where Callie got burned. It's off Top Trail on the east ledge."

Now Mr. Bean did have a surprised face. "You mean to tell me those l'il rascals went that far from home by themselves?"

I looked at Sandy, but he didn't seem to know how to help me put Mr. Bean onto how it was. "Coyt and Callie know their way 'round this mountain real good," I told him. "I'll take you there if you want."

The phone rang. It was Aunt Lou, and she was fit to be tied. Pa and Wylie were there, so she knew everything we did. "Don't go no place else till the whole caboodle of us get together at the church, " she told me. "We got to pray for direction."

"She's right," Sandy said when I gave him the message. "Before we scatter out, we need to ask God to guide us. Let's go there now."

"N-no," Mr. Bean argued. His voice was shaky, scared. "My babies are out there by themselves. Every minute counts."

One of Sandy's big powerful arms went around Potter Bean's shoulder. "I promise you, Potter, no time's wasted by asking God's help. Making the church a central point will help us organize a better search."

I could tell Mr. Bean wasn't so sure about all that, but I reckon he couldn't buck the ones whose help he needed.

Shortly, we were all together at the log chapel, holding hands. Sandy's prayer was short, but plenty big and then some. "Dear Lord," he prayed, "in Matthew 18:19 You tell us if two of us on earth agree about anything we ask for, Your Father in heaven will do it. You know we must find these little ones. We thank You for keeping them safe until You lead us to them."

The menfolk split into two groups. Sandy, Wylie, and I were to head up to the hermit hut. Pa and Mr. Bean planned to cover Miz Lizzie's tree farm and on down to the cottage sites.

"I've already checked with the night watchman at the big construction site," said Wylie. "He claims he's seen no one since he went on duty tonight."

That figured. If that beer-guzzling Hale was mixed up with Corn, he sure wasn't going to put himself out to help us.

Louise wanted to come along, but Pa said no, she was to stay with Ma and Aunt Lou. "And keep Midnight locked in there with you womenfolk," he ordered. "Wouldn't put it past that triflin' Corn Kelly to try and hide at the church."

"Humph," snorted Aunt Lou. "If'n he does, we'll make sure he'll wish he hadn't." Everyone could see she meant it.

It was plain that Wylie and Mr. Bean had not heard about Corn till then. "Are you talking about the man who once lived where we do?" Mr. Bean frowned. "Mr. Byall told me he was doing time for growing marijuana." His dark eyes got scared. "What if he got ahold of my children!"

Pa waved both hands without moving his elbows. "There ain't nary call for you to go gettin' upset over old Corn. He's big and scary-looking, but not likely to harm two l'il younguns."

I clamped my mouth together to keep it shut. In no way did I agree with Pa. When I was little, the big tobacco-spitting bully took extra pleasure in scaring the daylights out of me.

The chance that prison might have changed Corn was about as fat as a starved grasshopper. The whole idea of two little younguns meeting up with him at night purely gave me the creeps.

Just before we left, I heard Sandy ask Louise, in a low voice, to phone the sheriff's office so they would know we were looking for two little children.

Pa and Sandy had their guns along. "Whichever party finds the younguns, fire two shots in the air," Pa decided.

Midnight tried to follow us out. "Stay with Aunt Loooh!" I told him. He tucked his long black tail between his legs and gave me a sad, mournful look as I closed the door on him.

Our team covered the east side of the mountain first. We called Coyt and Callie every few steps we took. The beams from our flashlights fanned out ahead of us. We aimed them into every bush and hollow along our way, and in crevices between the rocks. But we didn't see or hear the twins.

No one was at the hut, so we went all over that side of the mountain for hours and hours, calling and hoping.

The day had been a long one, and it looked like we were in for a long night. I was plumb worn out. How good it would have been to crawl into my nice, clean bed. But there was no time for sleep. The twins were out there somewhere in the night— cold, scared. Criminals were out there too. No matter how dark it was, the search had to go on.

18
Lost Treasure

In TV movies, when somebody's lost on a rugged mountain, they put off an all-out search till morning. But us Finlays are not put together like that. When something or somebody is lost, we don't wait around for daybreak.

It was past midnight when we found ourselves back at the Beans' driveway, and Sandy said, "Someone should stay at the bus, in case the twins come home."

None of us could figure out why nobody thought of that before, especially Wylie. "I got too busy and forgot them," he said. "I'll never forgive myself if . . ."

"Don't blame yourself," Sandy interrupted. "Things like this just happen. And don't worry. We'll find them."

A light was on in the Beans' bus, and we found the door locked from inside.

My heart almost stopped. Had the twins come home, or was Corn Kelly with them in the bus?

"CALLIE! COYT! OPEN UP!" Wylie yelled.

It was Louise who opened the door. "They're not

here," she said. "Aunt Lou sent me and Midnight here to wait, just in case."

"Well, where *is* that mighty watchdog?" I asked.

She shrugged. "He took off soon as I stepped inside. Wouldn't come when I called, so I just locked myself in. Hey, you would not believe what a cozy little home this bus makes."

"We might if you let us inside," I said weakly.

Wylie shook his head. "N-not now, Johnny. Sorry, but I just can't stop looking."

"Well, you'll do better with some coffee to warm your insides," Louise told him. "I just brewed up a fresh pot in your coffee maker."

It might have been the good smell of coffee that made Wylie change his mind. But more likely, it was because he just naturally turned to putty in my sister's hands. "I reckon we can stop for a minute," he decided. Sandy and I didn't argue.

We huddled over a table behind the driver's seat. Sandy asked Louise if she had seen Pa and Mr. Bean.

"Not in the half-hour I been here. Sounded like them calling 'mongst Miz Lizzie's trees."

Louise was right about how nice the bus was fixed up. No space was wasted. Two bunks lined the side walls, and we washed our hands in a tiny closet sink beside a john.

The back end was closed off by a sliding curtain. A sign saying LADIES ONLY was pinned on it. I could just see Callie's bright face as she whirled in that red-checked skirt. I bit my lip.

"We're not leaving Louise here alone," Sandy announced to Wylie and me.

"I'm not scared," Louise said. "This place is secure enough to protect the most precious treasures."

Something clicked in my head. "Sandy, you stay here with Louise. I know my way along them woods and high rocks back there."

"You're right, Johnny. Louise, did you call the sheriff?"

"I did, and he said there wasn't much they could do till sunup, but a chopper's already set to come then to hunt for Corn Kelly. Said Mr. Byall okayed them parking a mobile unit at the construction site."

"We might need to do some climbing around them rocks," I said. "Won't take long to get the twins here when we find 'em." I tried to sound confident. "Then Sandy can shoot the good news in the air."

Soon we were all over the woods behind the Bean place, calling and hoping.

"I wish Louise hadn't called the sheriff," Wylie said when we had almost reached the line of rocks.

"Wylie, Louise didn't have no choice. We need lots of help."

"Yeah, and most likely Human Services will see that we get their brand of it. They'll say Dad's not a fit parent and go put Coyt and Callie in a foster home like before."

"Before?"

For a minute, the only sound was our sneakers kicking against stones. Then Wylie said, "The time our mom got custody of me and the babies. Even after she'd gone off and left us to root hog or die, she got around that judge."

"How'd she do that?"

"Mom was a charmer. Got 'im believing she was over being mind-sick—that she was fit to be a better parent than Dad was."

"Are your parents divorced?"

"Yep. That's when it happened. Wasn't long 'fore Mom left us again. She'd leave us for a day or two at a time." He sighed. "I was nine when she ran off with a boyfriend. D-Dad says it wasn't anything we did—she just couldn't cope with responsibility."

We called the twins again. Still no answer.

"But how'd you get to be in a foster home, Wylie?"

"After Mom left that last time, I couldn't reach Dad right off. Some snitch of a neighbor phoned Human Services. Right away, I got thrown into one foster home and the twins in another. When Dad found out, he got full custody of us, and we been with h-him ever since." I could tell he was crying. "I'll n-never forgive myself if—"

"Don't say if, Wylie. Back at the church, there's

some powerful praying going on. Miracles happen when Aunt Lou gets a prayer chain going."

"I'm sorry I got onto you like I did for you coming to our place with Mr. Carroway. You Christians are okay folks. Reckon maybe I need to know the Lord better, myself."

"Stick around, then," I said. "We'll see to it."

We bounced our lights off the line of rocks all the way to where the creek cut fast and deep underneath the high rock wall. Like I figured, only a fool would try to swim under it to the other side.

We turned back, still calling through the darkness.

It was chicken-hollering time when we got to the tree I had climbed, and I heard a dog bark. A picture ran across my brain—Midnight and the twins.

With two fingers over my mouth, I whistled.

"Midnight!" I called, and whistled again.

Like some phantom of morn-gloam, Aunt Lou's dog appeared beside the line of boulders just ahead of us.

He kept running back and forth from us to where he had come out. You would have thought he'd treed a coon.

"He's probably after a rabbit," Wylie said.

"I don't think so. Midnight wouldn't fetch me to help him chase a little ole rabbit. Let's go see."

When he saw we were almost there, the dog squeezed through a narrow gap between two rocks.

The hole was too little for us to follow, but Midnight didn't notice that. He kept poking his head out, urging us on. Then it hit me. If Midnight could get through that crack, so could the twins.

"We got to find a way to follow that dog," I said. "He's on to something."

I got on my knees and flashed my light through the crack as far as I could. Its glow touched something blue. "Wylie, what color dress was Callie wearing?"

He wasn't sure. "Green, no, blue." He took a look and got excited. "That's a scrap from her dress, all right. CALLIE! COYT!"

Nobody answered. "Probably asleep," I said, hoping I was right.

"We've got to get over these rocks," Wylie said.

For once, I managed to do some straight thinking. From where we were, I figured that camper was just opposite us, on the other side of the high boulders. I couldn't tell whether or not Wylie knew about the camper, but if he didn't, there was no need to upset him more by telling him now. It looked like the twins might have found a way through the rocks. If the worst had happened, it was better for me to find out first.

"Wylie," I said, "if you hoist me high as you can, I think I can make it over that high rock."

The rocks were at least twice taller than I was. But a jagged piece stuck out at the top of one of them. If I could get high enough to reach for it, maybe I could latch on. After Wylie held me by my sneaker soles and gave me two or three hard pushes, I made it.

I crash landed into a thick bed of leaves that had drifted in there and gotten trapped. Over me was the half-moon in a gray morning sky. Around me was a solid wall of rocks. Across from the crack Midnight had come through, I faced a larger opening. The dog pounced in and out of it like he was saying, "this way, buster." That opening was plenty big enough for me to crawl into.

I picked up the scrap of Callie's blue dress and could almost hear her saying, "We got lots of playhouses." Now I knew I should have told Wylie about the silver spoon. If he had known, he might have kept all this from happening.

By now, I didn't think Wylie nor Mr. Bean knew beans about the twins' "hidden treasure."

"It looks like a cave," I told Wylie as I passed him the dress scrap. "You wait there. I'm going in."

"Okay, but make sure you don't run out of light in there."

"Gotcha." I could see why Coyt guarded his flashlight. I couldn't see them crawling in a dark tunnel without one.

Midnight yanked me by the legs of my jeans as I put new batteries in my flashlight. Then I beamed it ahead of me and climbed into the hole.

Pa always said there were caves in those rocks. If

they hadn't been on Corn's corner of the mountain, I might have gone looking before now. It truly did appear that the Bean twins had got ahead of me again. I just hoped those gutsy little younguns were as tough as they thought they were.

Close places don't set too well with me, but that ole dog refused to let me halt one time. One second my light was on his snaky black tail, and the next it was mirrored in his shiny eyes. I was glad to find the tunnel was roomy enough for a full-grown man to crawl through, but it was curved around rocks, so there was no way to see the end of it.

YAP YAP, barked Midnight from ahead of me. He couldn't have been more than five feet away. Sooner than I counted on, his cold nose welcomed me at the other end.

I stood and breathed deep as I fanned my light around a big room with rock-studded walls and ceiling. At the far end, a shaft of gray morning light seeped into the cave. It cut through shadows to show me what was in the room.

I was looking at about a half dozen TV sets, stereos, and the like. Big boxes were everywhere.

Midnight tugged at my jeans leg, then let go and dived between two tall boxes near the wall. I tailed him as fast as I could.

19
Treasure Found

The two tall boxes were alongside others, all jammed up close together. Midnight sniffed and gnawed at the corner of one of them. I poked around till I opened enough space in the wall of boxes to spot Callie's faded blue dress. But it wasn't moving. All I could hear was Midnight's low whining and the BOOMP BOOMP of my own heartbeat.

"Coyt? Callie?" No answer. Midnight whined louder. I latched onto the scruff of his neck to steady myself.

I pried another box loose and zigzagged it toward me. I didn't dare push, for fear of crushing the twins. Soon I had enough room to get through to them.

Midnight nosed ahead of me. He went straight to the twins. They were lying on a pile of old rags. Someone had tied up their hands and feet with strong twine. Their mouths were gagged with strips of rags. "Get back, Midnight," I said as I dropped to my knees beside them.

I laid my fingers over Coyt's nose, then Callie's. "Whew!" I sighed with relief. They were fast asleep, but alive, with dried-up dirt and tears streaking their cheeks.

It all clicked in my mind in a split second.

One. A rotten somebody had left these little younguns tied and gagged. Two. That somebody might show up any minute. Three. I had to get the twins outside to Wylie in a hurry.

Midnight woke them with a couple of his drooly good morning kisses, and I cut the twine loose with my pocketknife.

I had not forgotten how loud Callie could holler. I clamped my hand over the mouths of both of them. "Shhh," I said, "it's Johnny. You two all right?"

They were. And for once, they didn't buck me. "We wanna go home," Coyt whispered. Callie couldn't talk for sobbing, but she kept it down like I told her to. Midnight pushed in between us, licking their faces, making sure they were all right.

"Some men came to our treasure house," Coyt said real low. "They talked mean, and I kicked one of 'em. Then they tied us up for months and months."

I got them through the tunnel into the little rock-circled room outside. Then they squeezed through the crack and into their brother's open arms.

Over his little sister's sobs, I heard Wylie's happy voice. "I never thought I'd be so glad to see you guys! What's wrong, Callie?"

Three sobs in a row. "I—I wet my pants," she told him. Through the crack, I could see Wylie hugging her real tight, saying it was okay.

Coyt got right back to being his cocky self. "I wasn't a bit scared," he bragged, "but what took y'all so long?"

Now that the twins were okay, I filled Wylie in on my suspicions about the camper and the boxes in the cave. "You take the twins and tell Sandy to fire the gun," I told him. "I'm going back to look into some of those boxes."

"But how you gonna get out?"

"I'll sneak out the other side, less'n Pa can get here with ropes before the bad guys start stirring."

When Midnight saw I wasn't going, he squeezed back through the opening. "No, Midnight," I told him. "You been braver'n I ever figured you to be. Go on with the others now!" He cocked his head to one side, but went on after I gave him a sound whack to make a believer out of him.

I took a deep breath and snuck back into the cave. It was still quiet. I shone my flashlight in a circle around the room. Then I opened a box near the tunnel entrance. It was filled with fine-looking odds and ends, packed in white foamy balls that looked like snow. I dug down into it, and pulled out Miz Lizzie's silver spoon with a W on it.

I had seen enough. Now all I could think about

was finding out who was staying in that camper.

More light was coming in from outside. I made my way to the cave entrance and stepped through a hole about six feet high. About three feet out, heavy brush was piled higher than the opening. I could see through the brush, but it hid me and the entrance from the outside world. I peeped down through the morning mist.

A makeshift trail of big tire marks zigzagged about 300 yards downward between rocks. It was just wide enough for vehicles to drive up to the pile of brush. Further down, the tire marks disappeared into a thicket of tall willows and other bushy trees. From the camper, anyone who didn't know about the uphill trail might never notice it was there. It was plain that the thieves figured they had a foolproof setup on my mountain. But I was doing some figuring of my own.

I sat behind the brush like a coon in a hollow log, and waited.

20
Haul Buggy or Bust

The time was right for Wylie and the twins to be getting back to the bus. When they did, Sandy would fire two shots. Wherever they were, that would bring Pa and Mr. Bean hurrying toward the Bean place. Then Pa would bring a rope or something to fetch me out of the little outdoor room at the end of the tunnel.

I started thinking. Maybe Pa and I would be heroes. Maybe he would get over the rocks and the two of us would sneak down to the camper together and surprise the sleeping thieves. I got tingly with excitement.

On the other hand, maybe the night watchman was the only one who stayed at the camper. What if Hale rolled up in his dirty white pickup and surprised Pa and me poking around his camper. We would have to be careful.

BANG BANG! Two shots echoed down the mountainside. It meant the twins were home safe.

Soon Pa would come and bring a rope to pull me to safety too.

In a flash, I saw the door of the camper swing open. A skinny man wearing nothing but boxer shorts stumbled sleepily from the door.

That mud-brown beard and pigtail could belong to nobody but Boozer. He growled something I couldn't hear to somebody in the camper.

A big bear of a man might near dropped like a bomb from the same door. His drab coveralls were all wrinkled like he'd slept in them. Icy squiggles rose from my stomach to my throat. It was Corn Kelly.

But that wasn't all. After Corn, out jumped a young, muscular black man, wearing jockey shorts.

Well, shucks a mile and then some! It was none other than Tyrell, who played the blues on his harmonica; the same "nice young man" Miz Lizzie had let come into her house to use the phone. What a neat way for him to see she had something worth stealing!

Aunt Lou has always said it's good to have good manners, but it takes more than that to make you good. I could just see Tyrell's van backing up to Miz Lizzie's kitchen door right after she and Biltmore left to buy groceries.

The men were looking up toward the cave entrance, shaking their heads and arguing. Then another noise sent them scuttling for cover under the willows.

A helicopter was riding the air up the mountain. Treetops flattened out in its path. It had to be the sheriff's helicopter, clattering toward Byall's landing pad.

Soon as the helicopter was out of sight, the men came out again. Then Corn went into a slow trot, stumbling as fast as he could up the slope toward the cave.

I backed inside. For a bit of a minute, I thought of crawling back through the tunnel. But Pa needed more time to get to me. If the men came to the cave, I'd be a sitting duck in the little rock room, for certain. I had to hide fast, but where? I looked around.

Near the entrance were some big boxes. One of them lay sidelong, a heavy one that was reinforced with wood slats. I peeped inside. Except for a lot of balled-up packing paper, it was empty. Outside, I could hear Corn Kelly cursing as he pulled back the pile of brush. I had no time to lose.

Faster than a lizard in a henhouse, I backed into the box. Pushing the wads of paper in front of me, I slid back as far as I could. Hunkered back on my sneakers, I prayed that my hideout was a safe one.

I heard Corn stomp past me and over to where the twins had been tied up. What comments he blurted out would not bear repeating.

Pa always said his old partner was meaner than he was smart. Now, I wondered how long it would be till he figured that whoever freed the twins might still be in the cave. I swallowed and hoped he didn't hear it like I did.

Someone else was pushing the brush aside. "Got doughnuts and coffee, Corn. And a pack 'uh paper cups." It was Tyrell's voice. He halted in front of my hiding box, with Boozer stopping behind him. I got a whiff of perked coffee. My box shook as Tyrell set the pot down on top of it. I could hear the shu-shu-shu of plastic wrapped doughnuts being opened. What a dumb hiding place I'd picked.

"Grove oughta be here soon," Boozer remarked. "Hope he's got some ideas about haulin' this stuff to Nashville right away. We can't turn them younguns loose till we unload it."

Grove. Sam Grove? Not Hale, the night watchman, but Grove, the foreman? Uh-HUH.

The two men were so close, I could have untied Tyrell's athletic shoes or pulled the long red hairs on Boozer's skinny legs.

"Hey, Corn," yelled Tyrell. "You gonna untie them younguns' hands so's they can eat a doughnut?"

No answer.

"Still sleepin', huh?"

Corn sure knew a lot of cuss words. "Gone," he sputtered in the middle of a string of them. "The brats got loose." He swore again.

Now it was Boozer using x-rated words. He

banged into the corner of my box getting back to where Corn was.

"I told you, Booze," Corn said in his raspy voice, "this stuff oughta been hauled off last night when I got here." The heavy man hadn't stopped panting from hurrying uphill.

"Grove didn't think so," Boozer reminded him. "Said Tyrell was too late startin' up the mountain with his van full of loot last night."

Things were hitching together for me. The foreman at the Byall construction site was also the boss of the theft ring! Or maybe Will Byall was the secret top man, with Sam Grove the go-between. Was the water-bottling plant going to be a front for criminal activity?

Corn stomped over, and I could hear the sound of coffee being poured. "No foolin', Booze. We don't need no boss who lets his wife run him." Slurp slurp, went Corn. "I don't owe Sam Grove nothing. He didn't spring me like he did you and Tyrell."

I took a deep breath and held it till I heard a hand going back into the doughnut package. The sweet smell seeping through the cracks made my mouth water.

"It was you, Corn, that sent us to this place," spoke up Tyrell. "Sam Grove just saw to it we was hired to work on the buildings. You swore nobody'd ever find this cave, that you was the only one what knew about it."

113

Corn coughed. "And I was. How'd I know some dad-ratted younguns was gonna squeeze through a crack in the rocks?"

"Hmmmm." It was Boozer studying things out. "Them twins are two little toughies. You s'pose they untied themselves?"

Corn coughed again, then swore. "Nothing I tie up gits loose less'n a rat helps 'em."

"Grove said we'd take 'em along on the haul—for insurance," Boozer said. "He ain't gonna be happy over this."

"Maybe my big haul last night will sweeten his bread," said Tyrell. "See that big CD player over there? And I got some of the craziest, mixed-up paintings, the kind you get big money for. I been countin' on makin' it to Nashville." He cracked his knuckles. "Soon's I cut me a record, I'm goin' straight."

"If you'd come in earlier last night, we might be halfway there with a van full of loot by now," barked Boozer. "Now a chopper's out looking for us, and we got no hostages for a getaway."

Nobody answered. I figured it had not yet dawned on dumb old Corn that I might still be around. When it did, I was going to be in a fix and a half.

"JOHNNY ELBERT!" It was Pa, calling me from beyond the tunnel. Oh boy. Here I was right under the enemy. If only I had hid in the little rock room.

But if I had, I might not have found out that Sam Grove was the leader of the theft ring. Now I just hoped I'd live to tell it.

"Let's get outta here!" Tyrell's voice sounded scared. "I don't want to go back to prison."

"Not so fast," said Boozer. "That man was calling 'Johnny.' So somebody named Johnny must still be in this cave."

"Earle Finlay's boy, Johnny!" Corn's voice was full of anger.

"Man, let 'im be," Tyrell said. "Let's just split. I know a place away from this mountain where we can hide till all this blows over."

"Then what?" Boozer asked. "We got too much at stake here. The boy can be our insurance. And if he's heard all we been saying, he knows too much."

My heart fairly jumped into my neck, then split and popped out both ears. The men had put down their coffee cups and were stomping all over the cave, looking for me.

"Johnny Elllll-ber-r-t," Corn called, keeping his voice down low. "You remem-mm-berrr me, don'tcha, boy? You the one caused ole Corn to go to prison. Caused him t' lose all he had, you did. Gonna cost ya." His loud, raspy cough bounced off the cave walls. "Reckon as how we might take you for a leetle ride, boy. Might just drop yer off the Green River bridge. Yeh, I hear tell it's the highest bridge around these here parts."

"Aw, knock it off, man," Tyrell said. "You know you ain't gonna do nothing like that to a youngun. Not as long as I'm around." Which made me breathe a mite easier. Maybe there was some good in Tyrell, after all. But he was in bad company, and I couldn't trust him.

The scraping sounds of boxes being shoved about came from the tunnel side of the cave.

"I know you're in this here room, Johnny Elbert," Corn's voice was scratchy like sandpaper. "You might's well come on out."

All of the men were still on the other side of the cave.

I heard Boozer say, "We ain't got no more time to waste. I just stuck my head in that tunnel and heard some men talking. Heard one say somebody was bringing a ladder. They'll soon be over them rocks."

"I say we forget that boy and git while the gittin's good," said Tyrell.

"What about Grove?" Boozer asked.

"Yeh, what about 'im? He'll just know we split. Let him worry. He so loves being the big boss." Tyrell's voice sounded nearer.

"I say we go, soon's we check them empty boxes near the door," said Boozer.

I had heard enough. Footsteps were coming my way. I got out and picked up the end of the box. Hot coffee, milk, and doughnuts slammed through the air. I backed through the entrance and blocked it

116

with the big box. I hoped that would slow them down long enough for me to get a head start down the mountainside.

Without taking time to look back, I crashed through the brush pile. I was halfway down the slope before I heard the three men coming after me, running and swearing.

So far, I had not seen any weapons on the thieves. But if they were armed, Pa would be too. If only I could get to where he was, I knew I'd be home safe. But I was cut off from him by the line of tall rocks that went all the way to Mirror Rock Road.

I didn't know exactly where to run, only that I didn't plan on being caught. Corn was slow and clumsy, but not Boozer and Tyrell. I speeded up.

Without slowing, I headed down the makeshift drive into a willow thicket. Low limbs brushed me till I slammed into the back of a vehicle. It was Tyrell's dark grey van. I bounced off it and plowed through the willows as fast as I could. Then I kept running down the driveway that twisted through the woods to Mirror Rock Road.

I took a quick look back. I could see only Boozer coming after me. Still in his boxer shorts, his long legs were cutting down the space between us. Boozer was getting closer.

I was almost to Mirror Rock Road when I heard the motor of a vehicle cranking up. It had to be Tyrell's van. Now I would have a van to outrun too.

21
Ain't Over
Till It's Over

It's not easy to get your bearings when you're running for dear life. But I knew where the creek was. It took a piece of a second to decide to swing that way. Which was how long it took Boozer to gain five feet more on me.

I heard Tyrell's van stop behind him.

"Git 'im, Booze," hollered Corn. "Haul 'im back here to the van."

What I had over Boozer was knowing how to run in a mountain woods. Corn might think and tell him to head me off at the creek, but that was a chance I had to take.

About the same time I ran splashing into the shallow creek, the sheriff's chopper whirred loudly overhead.

Jumping up and down, I waved my arms and hollered near about to heaven. The chopper hovered a second, then dropped a flare on the bank near me. Then it putter-putted toward Mirror Rock Bridge.

I looked back. No Boozer, no Corn. But I knew they weren't far away, only out of sight. My best hope was to keep to the creek, clear of the trees. Jumping from slippery rock to slippery rock, I headed toward the bridge.

When the bridge came in sight, I saw two patrol cars parked beside it. Two deputies stood on the bridge, and two were coming along the creek bank toward me. I ran to meet them, all the time pointing to the place Scott said he saw car tracks turning into the woods.

"Van a'comin'," I held up three fingers. "Thieves! (pant-pant). Tell-men-on-bridge-BLOCK THAT VAN!"

Seeing I was safe now, the patrolmen got right on their radios. The patrol cars stopped Tyrell's van just before it pulled onto Mirror Rock Road.

Right after that, Pa, Sandy, Wylie, and Mr. Bean showed up. When they didn't find me in the cave, they followed the creek bank to the bridge.

I purely enjoyed hearing those thieves' rights read to them.

"Reckon maybe I been listening to the wrong people," Tyrell said before they got into the patrol car. As it hauled them off, he was the only one of the three who waved directly at me.

I have to say Corn was direct too though. He raised his handcuffed fists. I could read his snarly lips saying, "I'll git you for this, you l'il devil!"

I believed him for about a minute, till Pa's strong arms hugged me tight. Then I knew Corn had gone and told a big old lie.

There is something else I know for a fact and a whole lot more. God looks after His children real good.

22
Sharing Mirror Mountain

A week or so later, there was a big celebration at the log chapel. All the congregation was there. Scott and Willis came with their families. Sandy McRee brought Jenny Blair, my last year's teacher. Each of them thinks the other one hung the moon.

Corn Kelly was taken straight back to prison, which was where he got tangled up with Boozer and Tyrell in the first place. Sam Grove had been their boss before that, for legal and illegal jobs. But he hadn't been caught, and they never squealed on him. For that, Grove helped them get early paroles and new building jobs, and they went right back to stealing for him.

But this time, Sam Grove didn't come out smelling like a rose. No, siree. This time, Tyrell and Boozer told all I had heard in the cave, and a whole lot more. Most likely, old Grove will soon be eating prison rations too.

As for Hale, turns out he's just a grouchy man who's ruining his health by smoking cigarettes and guzzling beer. Sandy says we need to pray for him and show him a little kindness.

I was glad for all this, except for Tyrell. I really liked him. But I reckon I found out for certain that liking a person doesn't necessarily mean you can trust him. Maybe, when he gets out, Tyrell really will take his blues songs to Nashville and go straight. Could be we'll hear him singing "Mirror Mountain Blues" on one of those country music TV shows one day. Some really bad songs turn out to be hits. You never know.

Sandy had invited Mr. and Mrs. Will Byall to our party too, which did not please me at all. No matter how smiley-nice the couple acted, I felt obliged to distrust any man who sat back and let his workmen chop up our mountain. I was sorely vexed to see everyone shaking Byall's hand like he was something wonderful. Didn't anyone else care that Balmy Springs might dry up? Pa caught the question in my eye, but he only winked like he knew some big secret I didn't.

Then Sandy got up and said how great it was that Mr. Byall was building a Christian retreat on North Road.

I tell you for a fact, what I heard took the whole biscuit with honey oozing out! And it was true, because Sandy McRee does not lie. I just stood there in a daze for a second or so. Then I opened my mouth and praised the Lord right along with everybody else.

"Now we know that Balmy Springs won't dry up," Sandy said. He went on to allow that even if it ever did go dry, the Lord would go right on looking after His people like always. He reminded us of what Jesus told the woman at the well in the Book of John, "Whoever drinks the water I give him will never thirst."

Mr. Byall told the whole roomful of people that he knew God had led him to our beautiful mountain. "He called me to provide a quiet place close to nature—a place where Christians might meet and worship together." He said it was a real inspiration to see how mountain folks helped each other.

But I had a bit of a bone to pick with that rich man. After he finished talking, I went over and shook his hand. Then I told him I planned to be a conservationist, and how disturbed I was to see so many trees being torn down. He said he felt the same way. He gave me his word that there would be no more unnecessary tree cutting. Since then, he's been up here every day, keeping that promise.

The church has its sound system back. Miz Lizzie is back to polishing silver, and proudly shows a picture Willis took of Biltmore standing beside the Civil War rifle. She has pretty much taken Coyt and Callie under her wing, which is a miracle to behold. She's spoiling those younguns rotten, but they've stopped running wild. They don't leave home without Wylie's say-so.

As for Miz Lizzie's yard tools, well, nobody stole them. Biltmore owned up to hiding them under some bushes at the back of the tree farm. He said he needed some time off from tending Christmas trees and cleaning up the yard, which was true enough.

That was why Wylie and I helped him give that yard a cleaning it would not forget. We even cut down bushes Miz Lizzie had not planned on doing away with. She said we did such a good job, she wouldn't need our help again for some time to come. Then, to show her appreciation, she served us up a good meal.

Mr. Bean has started coming to church with his family. Pa and the other men are helping him finish building the kiln for his pottery. After that, they're going to help him build a real house for his family.

Although he's too busy to meet with us every time, Wylie is now a Hermiteer. Scott, Willis, and I meet at the hermit hut right regular since both of their families bought vacation cottages down below Miz Lizzie's.

When I go over all the changes that have taken

126

place, I figure we mountain folks won't get the short end of the stick by a long shot. I reckon the Lord made Mirror Mountain plenty big enough to hold a passel of good people.